# IN A HEART BEAT

By

I0691276

## C. A. King

Cover Design:

Jennifer Munswami
–
J.M. Rising Horse Creations

Editor:

Karen Hrdlicka

*If you believe this book is dedicated to you,*

*perhaps it is!*


*Look for other books by C.A. King, including:*

*The Portal Prophecies:*
*Book I – VI*
*Volume I & II*

*Tomoiya's Story:*
*Book I: Escape to Darkness*
*Book II: Collecting Tears*

*Surviving the Sins:*
*Book I: Answering the Call*
*Book II: Pride*
*Book III: Lust*
*Book IV: Gluttony*
*Book V: Wrath*

*Flower Shields: A Four Horsemen Novel*

*Drawing Strength From Words: A Four Horsemen Novel*

*Hitting The High Note: A Four Horsemen Novel*

*When Leaves Fall: A Different Point of View Story*

*Peach Coloured Daisies: A Cursed by the Gods Story*

*Miracles Not Included*

*Twisted Tales of A Dead End Street*

*Shot Through The Heart: A Faerie Tale*

*Do Not Open Until Halloween*

*Truly Unfortunate*

*Serendipity's Debt*

*Hope After Death*

*Merry Apocalypse*

*Cupid's Connection*

*Cover Design:* **Jennifer Munswami - J.M. Rising Horse Creations**

*First Printing: July 2019*

*ISBN: 978-1-988301-86-0*

*Kings Toe Publishing*

*kingstoepublishing@gmail.com*

**Brantford, Ontario. Canada**

# *Chapter One*

Immortality was boring. That wasn't just a statement; it was the plain truth. While some point during the last century had given birth to the glorification of the dead, or undead, depending on how one looked at it, what played on the big screen was nothing more than a big, fat lie. Fancy monster parties that lasted until the wee hours of the morning were nothing more than wishful thinking. Vampires didn't sparkle and they also didn't continually attend high school. There were no special academies hidden away in some magical corner of the world that hadn't yet been explored. And, most importantly, a god wasn't coming to save anyone's soul. Demon, vampire, shifter, or human—it was up to each to find their own way in the world.

After the first hundred years or so, simply existing began to feel like a chore. Since everything had been tried more than once, there were simply no thrills left to be had. That was when any immortal found themself faced with a choice; continue to endure or drift off into an eternal sleep. Eternal probably wasn't the right word. Slumber parties usually only lasted a few centuries; just long enough to let the world grow and change. Those wakening found themselves in whole new lands. As enticing as that plan was, it also wasn't convenient in many ways. It wasn't as if an eternal could lie down and snore through the ages in plain sight. In most cases, it involved faithful servants and relying on their bloodlines to be equally as dedicated.

Remaining awake wasn't a piece of cake either. The mind easily became as dead as the soul when not challenged. The key to surviving became mastering the ability to keep one piece of humanity tucked away in a pocket. Sentiments were exactly what any doctor would order, after they finished freaking out over the whole not-living part. The problem was, the longer one existed, the less attached to feelings they became. A strong emotion was needed to keep two feet in the mortal world. There weren't a lot of those to choose from.

The first thing everyone thought of was always love, and with good reason. It was undeniably the most intense of its kind. It also wasn't a feasible choice. No one chose whom they fell in love with. It simply happened or it didn't. More often it was the latter. There was another option, though. It didn't require any hard work to achieve; was easily reproduced when needed; and could be hung onto for long periods of time. Anger was the perfect answer.

If anyone ever wondered where the evil label, which had been attributed to a large portion of the supernatural population, came from, that was the answer. Rage was an immortal's last connection to the living world.

Seth put down his pen. That was enough reflection for one day. He still wasn't sure writing a journal solved any of his problems, but the self-help tapes all insisted it did. With the hype over vampires that had spawned in the media the last couple of decades, anyone who found his scribblings would assume he was working on a book or movie script, rather than a strange memoir.

He glanced at his watch. It was time. The sun was down and he was more than a little famished. The first stop was going to be the twenty-four-hour drugstore. The need to fill time over the years meant night classes and more recently, Internet lessons. Chemistry, nutrition, and even some unconventional theories all had his mind reeling. The result: he spent the past five years proving that his kind didn't actually have to drink blood. It was the pure nutrients the life fluid contained they craved. With a bit of experimentation he managed to create a perfect mix of minerals, irons, and vitamins in a liquid form. There was no one to share his findings with, though. Even if there were, he doubted they'd be interested. The thrill of the kill was almost as satisfying as the anger behind the deed. Being able to feel was the one thing he couldn't duplicate in a pharmacy.

He tossed a twenty down on the counter to pay for his supplies. The man behind the counter side-eyed the pentagram mark on his wrist.

"Michael," Seth said, glaring at the name tag on a white uniform. "Thank you for all your help." A playful wink acted as an exclamation mark to his words.

"My pleasure," the man lied.

Seth chuckled under his breath. That was a typical human. They had no idea how bad they reeked when they spewed about untruths. It was worse than smelling morning breath on the train during the morning commute. More than half the daily riders had no clue what a toothbrush was or how to use it.

He glanced back at Michael, deciding to give the kid a one-time pass. The night was young, and someone else was sure to get under his skin a tad more before it was over.

A lopsided grin inched over his face. Bag in hand, he headed back to his car to fix dinner. A few sips were all he needed to rejuvenate his strength. Keys jingled in his hand, ready to open the lock. The cold of steel pressed against his temple froze him where he stood. He'd chosen a parking spot hidden in the back of the building on purpose.

"I'll take those," a gruff voice demanded, snatching the keys. "And the wallet. Take it out slowly. Any sudden moves and you're a dead man."

"Just my luck," Seth said, raising his hands. "I was looking for a fight." Before a grin could fully form on his face, the scuffle was over. He sighed, kicking the carcass by his feet. The bout hadn't lasted long enough to enjoy. There was no reward in taking scum off the street. He was no vigilante. His assailant's identification was something he could use, though. He stripped the man of anything useful, before dumping the body in a garbage bin.

The car door squeaked open, unwilling to be considered an accessory to the murder and knowing it wouldn't be the last one to happen that night. The engine purred to a stop in front of a local nightclub, where it was happy to remain parked for the rest of the eve. Seth stepped out, glancing over the line-up at the entrance. Twenty minutes for a beer was unreasonable in any day and age. Still, small towns were lucky to have any entertainment at all.

A group of girls, well under the drinking age, giggled as they strutted by. The bouncer ushered them in without glancing at a single poorly made fake ID. To have a line-up of paying men, a club needed ladies. This one, like most unscrupulous businesses in the area, didn't care about the safety of teens wanting to grow up a little too fast. Within a year at least one of their pretty faces would be a poster on the back of a milk carton. It was a wonder local authorities couldn't figure out why disappearances happened when it was as plain as day to everyone else.

Seth kept his thoughts private. He wasn't there for entertainment. A good old pub brawl was what he craved. The Big Red Bullet might have had a stupid name, but its parking lot was dimly lit and the perfect place to settle any score. There was nowhere better to pick a fight than a bar after hours.

A blood mint was exactly what he needed—another one of his home inventions. Each little tablet looked, smelled, and tasted the same as any breath freshener tablet on the market. His, however, contained just enough blood to get the juices flowing in his mouth. Dry mouth was one more on a long list of the cons of being a vampire.

A long string of drool dangled from him lips before landing on his new driver's licence. It wasn't a lot, but enough saliva to clean the image off with his sleeve. Even with the spit-shine, it looked a tad bit too new. Replacing pieces of identification came part and parcel with not ageing while the rest of the world did. The last set had him maturing just a smidge too much to remain believable.

Victims played double duty. From their ashes, he rebuilt a life for himself. Their pockets contained exactly what he needed to keep up the facade. He tore the blood from their veins, occasionally the limbs from their bodies, and the identification from their wallets. Taking different pieces apart and putting them back together with his likeness had become second nature. Practice made perfect, and over the years, there had been plenty of time to do just that.

He glanced around the room at the plethora of waste. Mortals filled every corner of the dance club. He could smell their lust oozing out, even over top of the stale beer and cheap cologne pockets that plagued such establishments. He paused at a half-wall, leaning against the ledge to watch loose women shake their wares, some falling out of outfits two sizes too small for their bodies. The prettiest girls always went to those with a few bucks extra in their wallets. As the night went on, those remaining would wear desperation as the only makeup capable of surviving sweat and tears. Those were the targets for the majority of the male patrons. None of them minded what the chick looked like. A few beers made everything seem better than it was. They were eager for a blowjob that wasn't served in a shot glass. It wasn't as if they were going to remember names or faces the next day, anyway. By closing time, not a dime needed to be spent in payment, either. The only drinks bought were for themselves.

Seth inhaled deeply; the scent of pot filled his nostrils. He chuckled under his breath, taking a swig from a bottle of beer. The humans around him had no idea. The high they caught off a joint, sex, or alcohol, was nothing compared to drinking the life out of a person until only a shell remained. That was a vampire's addiction, and if he let it run rampant, no one in the town would have lived to see the sunrise. Every now and then, the news reported about a massacre in one small town or another. A shoddy explanation, that didn't pan out as truth, was a dead giveaway that one of his kind had lost control. It might not have happened often, but when it did, his existence was threatened. If people knew vampires were real, they'd have to kill them. Destroying one's food source was never an ideal plan. Even if he tried not to feed on the living too much, someone had to make all the vitamins and additives for his smoothies. Once all the normal folks were gone, the vamps would be forced to turn on each other. Now, that would be some fun, for everyone but the victor. Imagine besting all the supernaturals and coming out on top, only to have no one to brag to and nothing left to eat. That poor creature's end would be a worse fate than any other experienced.

He licked his lips, all the thoughts about death and violence stirring up an insatiable hunger. A single beat restarted his heart, sending blood surging through his veins. A twinge of pain complained in one shoulder. There was a fine line between dead and undead. He'd left having a pulse a smidge too long. Thickened bodily fluids didn't like to be moved—hence the aching sensation. A few blood thinners in his next concoction would fix things back up. He felt a jab against his back. That wasn't an internal stab. He spun around.

"Watch where you're going," a man ordered. He tipped his cowboy hat to show off a full view of an angry leer. "Apologize and buy me a beer for my troubles, and I might let you go without a beating." He cracked his knuckles, flexing his biceps at the same time.

Seth gave him a once over. Testosterone oozed from his pores worse than grease from a teenager working the fry station at a local hamburger joint. Everything about him was over-the-top masculine from his well-worn jeans to the two-day stubble on his chin. He was either one of the finer male specimens worthy of a good fight, or compensating for something. Either way, Seth was about to find out.

"Why don't we take things outside?" Seth asked.

"Outside," the man repeated, chuckling. "I don't need to go anywhere to teach the likes of you a lesson or two." His grin expanded as a fist came down without warning.

Seth tilted his head from side to side, rubbing his jaw. A sucker punch was disappointing. That meant the guy was definitely overcompensating. Still, he couldn't allow a cheap shot to go unpunished, even if he did have to hold back on his real power. He rotated his sore shoulder a couple times, matching grin for grin.

"Have it your way!" Seth exclaimed, throwing a punch of his own. He pulled back in a test of strength to set the boundaries for the rest of the skirmish.

The stranger stumbled back a few steps, shaking his head. "Is that all you got?" he asked, laughing.

"Not by a long shot," Seth answered, his fist making a direct contact to the man's jaw. A tooth flew across the room as his body fell backward, smashing a table.

Regaining his footing, the man went for a football tackle takedown. Seth sidestepped the lunge, easily. The man skidded across the dance floor, sending the ladies screaming in all directions, limbs flailing. He pushed himself to his feet once more.

"Why, you little bastard!" he yelled. "I'm going to cut you in two for that." A blade popped open in his grasp. He pointed it at his enemy.

Seth stood up straight, watching the smile of a dead man creeping over his opponent's face. This fight was over. That cowboy had attended his last rodeo and he never even saw it coming. A fist landed square in his midsection, followed by an uppercut. The man stumbled, falling into yet another table.

"Freeze!" a deputy officer demanded, his gun alternating between being pointed at their heads. "This ain't no place for a brawl, boys. We're going to have to take you in. Come easy so this doesn't get any messier than it already is."

Seth sighed, his hands rising in the air. He'd made the cardinal mistake—getting caught fighting in public. He might have been an immortal, but he lived in their world and had no choice but to abide by their rules—at least until he could find a way to relocate with a new name and identity. It was too bad, too. He was starting to like it there.

"Don't move!" the deputy yelled, pulling Seth's arms behind his back one at a time. The cold smooth surface of metal clicked around each wrist. The handcuffs might have been shiny, but silver they weren't. He could have pulled them apart in a moment's notice, using only his pinky fingernail. That would have drawn too much attention, though. The other guy started the fight. Odds were Seth would end up with a warning and be cut loose within the hour.

"What we got here?" the sheriff asked, leaning against the doorframe to the establishment. He turned to spit on the sidewalk before fully entering. "A couple drunken delinquents?"

"A bar fight," the deputy answered. "We arrived before any real damage was done. I think you should take a gander at the other guy."

The sheriff strolled over to the man on his back on the ground. A baton lifted his chin. "What in the blazes, Roy?" He scolded. "You know your mamma and daddy ain't gonna like this."

# Chapter Two

The sheriff glanced through the cell's bars. "You boys are lucky the judge is going to hear your case before he leaves for the weekend. You could have been stuck here until Monday." His words ended in a chuckle.

Seth glanced down at his cuffed hands. They'd made the changeover from behind the back to front the moment they arrived at the jail. The other fellow had been released from his. Things were adding up the wrong way and that meant bad news. If Roy's father was a big shot in town, odds were any proceeding was going to head south quickly.

"On your feet," the sheriff ordered. "It's time to take the walk of shame." A black baton banged against the metal parts of prison doors.

Seth rose. Aggravating the local authority was counterproductive. He despised the way he was being treated. That frame of mind fed his building rage. In essence, the situation was serving its purpose. His heart had a steady beat. It wouldn't last long, though. Being in lock-up would grow old quickly with nothing to do. Rotting away in a cage was something he had no intentions of ever doing.

A jab in the back propelled him forward. The chuckle in his ear and hot breath on his neck were almost enough to push him over the edge. His fists tightened—knuckles turning white under the pressure. The deputy opened a set of double doors leading to the courtroom. Everything was all contained in one building—how convenient.

Seth had seen a lot of courts in his day, but this one was the most backwoods of them all. Full-length windows were covered by curtains made from flags—only some of which he recognized. That wasn't the kicker, though. Justice wasn't supposed to endorse religion. A large cross hanging behind the bench begged to differ. There was little doubt Christianity had a hand in all decisions set before this legal system.

"Sit," the sheriff ordered, pushing him back into a chair behind one of the two tables positioned facing a large wooden desk. "Roy, on the other side."

Roy took his place as instructed, holding his head down. "Is this really necessary? I won't press charges!" he offered.

"It's too late for that," the sheriff replied. "Besides, The Big Red Bullet has some damages to be taken care of. Who do you think is getting the bill?"

Roy's head sank further as the deputy announced Judge Thompson was presiding. He squirmed in his seat, chomping on what was left of his ragged nails.

"Thank you, deputy," the judge said, a fake grin plastered to his face. "What do we have here? Roy Thompson, what am I going to do with your sorry ass?"

"It wasn't me, Dad," Roy lied. "I swear it on Jake and Sissy's graves. That fella over there started it all. I was only defending myself."

"And not doing a good job of it at that," the judge scoffed. "Look at your face. You are a disgrace, boy. If your mother finds out, it's gonna break her sweet heart."

"Yes, sir," Roy agreed, holding his head up to show off his accused assailant's handiwork. "It was a right nasty sucker punch."

Seth's forehead wrinkled. This guy had to be joking. His black eyes were courtesy of the final hit, landing squarely on his nose. It clean broke it, and from the cracking noises, in at least two places to boot.

"You didn't see knuckles coming straight at you?" the judge argued. "This is a mess."

"I have witnesses," Roy blurted out. "They'll testify I was minding my own business when this guy decided to try to make a name for himself."

"Well," the judge said, rubbing the whiskers on his chin. "He sure managed to do that, didn't he? The question is, how to handle it..."

"Excuse me, your honour," Seth said, raising his still-cuffed hands. "Perhaps you'd like to hear my side of things?"

"Are you suggesting my boy is lying before the court?!" the judge bellowed, a small hammer banging down on the desk.

Seth shook his head. It wasn't even a proper gavel, but rather a common lightweight tool available at any hardware store. "I don't mean any disrespect, but there are several problems with this case. I wasn't charged or read my rights. I haven't been given access to legal representation or a chance to plead my case. I believe you will find just as many witnesses saw I didn't throw the first punch."

"Do you really think the citizens of this town will attest to such a thing in court?" the judge snickered. "We are a tight-knit group. We've been through a lot together... suffered losses." His eyes darkened. "Those sort of things leave scars and form bonds."

"No, I'd be foolish if I did," Seth admitted. "But that doesn't mean people haven't seen the truth. Eventually good folks will get tired of knowing the justice system is corrupt... especially where family matters are involved."

"He's got a point, Judge," the sheriff said, his tongue pushing a toothpick around his mouth. "People got to talking last time Roy got himself in trouble."

Judge Thompson took in a deep breath. "Neither one of you are getting off scott-free," he mumbled. "I want you both in anger management classes in the basement of the church, twice a week for the next six months."

Seth smiled, satisfied with the decision. He'd attend a meeting, maybe two; then disappear to forge a new existence in another town, preferably to the west. It had been a few decades since he'd been out that way. He held his hands out for his cuffs to be released; instead, the sheriff squatted before him. A single click took him be surprise. He glanced down at a contraption attached to his left ankle, colours flashing like an out-of-control traffic light.

"What's that?!" Seth yelled.

"That," the sheriff explained, chuckling, "is a tracker. We don't like sentence jumpers in these parts. We'll know if you try to leave town or skip out on a meeting."

"I know what you are thinking," the judge snickered. "I wouldn't try to remove it on your own. Only the correct combination to the lock and two keys can safely get rid of it. It was designed by an ex-explosives expert. If it is tampered with in any way... POOF." The judge used his hands to demonstrate the extent of the blast it would cause. "It would likely take that leg right off." He laughed. "Enjoy the classes."

Seth's jaw dropped. Anger management was the exact opposite of what he needed. Of course, going through the rest of time missing a limb wasn't a great option either. He'd messed up in the worst way possible.

# Chapter Three

It was a good thing vampires not being able to enter a church was one of the biggest lies of all time. Religion had a zero percent hold over on him. In fact, he'd spent a number of years studying as a monk, and even more living as a good old choirboy.

Various religious leaders were behind most spiritual myths. Throughout history, there were periods of time during which faith wore thin for one form of worship or another. Desperate times required severe actions. Tales of great feats, carried out in the name of a god against beasts and monsters from the bowels of the underworld, made religion great again. Fear brought congregations back together. It was world's first taste of sensationalism. Later it was all documented on the big screen.

Seth stopped short of the steps and a trio of smokers hanging out in front of the church entrance. Each one appeared to be in their mid-twenties, but none had yet grown out of being a teen. The blue-haired, shirtless male snarled at him as he made his way by; a chain running from his nipple piercing attached to his mate's collar. That wasn't the fellow's most noticeable attribute, though. That honour was left for the swear word spelled backward, tattooed to his forehead. It wasn't a far leap to realize what the word meant to read. Ink in this day and age was acceptable. Obscene language, however, was something most of society readily participated in, but still frowned on in public.

The second male dressed all in leather, kept his eyes focused down. He'd remain that way until his master said otherwise—a true submissive through and through.

"What are you staring at?" the female member of the group barked. She took another puff off her smoke, blocking the way into the church.

"I'm just doing my time," Seth said, motioning to their matching ankle accessories. "I'm rather fond of my leg." It wasn't a lie. He had no problems with tattoos—having several of his own—the most notable being a pair of folded angel wings covering his back. They appeared to be opening, but were forever frozen, much like his own life. People had their own reasons for ink and piercings. They also had their own preferences when it came to their sexuality. None of that was his to judge. Over the years he'd indulged in numerous forms of pleasure with men, women, and multiple partners. Love wasn't what made his world go round, feeling good was.

The girl laughed. Her sleeve became a tissue, wiping both her nose and smudges of black makeup smeared under her eyes. She moved to the side, bowing to grant him access to the class. "Watch out for old man Peters. If you ask me, he's the one who should be wearing this thing." She kicked her leg in the air. "You're early, by the way..."

Her words faded as the doors shut behind him. Seth glanced from side to side. There was no indication of which way led to the basement stairs. He passed through the greeting area and walls of empty hangers waiting for coats. A red carpet began at the farthest back pews. Some time had passed since he had entered any such building. It wasn't faith, or the lack there of, that kept him away. It was the self-righteousness of the men in charge that he despised. From the looks of things, not much had changed over the years. Decorations designed specifically to be humble in nature were never meant to be cast in solid gold. Seth shook his head, continuing his procession to the front altar and a cross that he had seen before. Either it was an exact duplicate of the one in the courthouse or vice versa.

"Can I help you?" a middle-aged priest asked, entering through a side door.

"I'm here for the meeting," Seth replied, spinning around. "It's my first visit to this parish, and I don't exactly know where I am supposed to be."

"It's commendable that you came early," the priest said. "I'm Father Peters. Follow me." He motioned toward a corridor that led to a steep staircase. At the bottom of the steps he paused. "I should mention this room used to be utilized by the congregation's youth group." He opened a door, ushering his new student inside.

A grin crept over Seth's face. If he had been anywhere else, he probably would have busted out in laughter. The room wasn't exactly youth friendly. It had been childproofed in every way possible, right down to the extra small sized chairs arranged in a circle.

"If you don't mind, it might be best if you wait until the others arrive before claiming a seat," Peters suggested. "Most of the attendees are creatures of habit. When dealing with explosive tempers, it is never wise to rock the boat."

"That's fine," Seth agreed. His plan was to be as cordial as possible and hopefully get rid of the thing on his ankle early. "I'm happy to stand if need be."

"That won't be necessary," Peters replied. "If one stands, everyone will want to. I have to keep some resemblance of order this evening."

"How many people are you expecting?" Seth asked. Idle chatter wasn't normally his thing, but something was needed to occupy the minutes before the session was scheduled to start. Sweat was already forming on his brow and this was only day number one. Normally, time didn't faze him. Centuries were only drops in the bucket for an immortal. These next six months, however, were going to be the longest he ever was forced to survive through. He tugged at his collar, feeling all the work he'd done to experience being alive wasting away. On the inside he was slowly dying again, literally. His heartbeats per minute had already reduced by half—circulation slowing to a crawl. Soon life would cease and he'd feel nothing again.

"Father," an elderly man slurred, staggering in the room. He looked and smelled as if a triple *A* meeting might have been more his pace.

"George," the priest replied. "You seem to have had a bit of a relapse. I wouldn't want to have to put a call into the sheriff."

George's fingers fumbled with his lips. A bit of foam formed in the corner of his mouth. An attempt to sit in a chair failed, he landed on his backside instead. "Who did that?!" he yelled, glancing around the room.

"You did, George," the priest answered, helping him up. "I'll get you some black coffee. You know the rules. You need to sober up before the meeting."

"I'm fine," George insisted, swatting in the air. "It was just a nip of brandy to warm the bones—nothing more."

"Hot coffee will warm you up just as well," Peters replied. "Stay put and try to stay out of trouble. That goes for both of you." He disappeared into the hallway.

Seth leaned against a wall, watching George argue with himself. He was a typical alcoholic through and through. For an immortal it made sense to behave in such a way. At least that's what they told themselves. Wasting decades of one's life in a fog of adrenaline rushes, that numbed the mind and body, meant little in a life that spanned eternity. For a mortal, though, it was sad. They had a finite number of years to enjoy all that life had to offer. Spending the majority of it in such a state meant missing out on so much more.

"Georgie!" another man exclaimed entering the room. "I got you a little something for after the meeting. Just you and me, like the gold ole days." He alternated pointing a finger between himself and George. His neck did a double take, the first glance back barely registering the presence of another person in the room. "And who might you be?"

"I'm the new guy," Seth answered.

"Well, the new guy." He used his fingers to make air quotations. "I'm Josh. I'm the *go-to* guy around here. This is Georgie. He's my best buddy."

"I'm Seth." He nodded, but kept his hands hidden in pockets.

"I'm the *go-to* guy," Josh repeated, pretending to throw a few punches in the air directly in front of Seth. "Get it? If you need something, I'm the guy you go to."

"Got it," Seth replied. "If I ever do need something, I'll... go to you."

"Perfecto! Muah." Josh kissed his fingers. "If you ever have an issue with Georgie, you come to me too. I'll make things right. We look out for each other."

Seth offered a weak smile. The evening wasn't off to a stellar start. So far, his companions for the next six months were a priest, a drunk, a junkie, and a guy who acted as if he desperately wanted to be part of the Italian Mafia, without being a part of that particular ethnic persuasion. It had all the elements needed for a really bad joke and he was the punchline. Of course, the thought of a vampire in the basement of a church, attending an anger management class, was hilarious on its own.

"Here we go," Peters said, returning with the coffee. "Nice and black. Josh, good to see you here again this week."

"I wouldn't miss it, Father," Josh said. "Maybe you could do that thing I like. You know... bless me before I go back out into the hard cruel world."

"We'll see at the end of the meeting," Peter's replied. "I trust you had an uneventful few days. I'd like to think your time spent with us has done some good."

"Oh yeah," Josh said. "I held back just like you taught me to. It wasn't easy, either. This guy stiffed me two bucks he borrowed for a coffee. The moron refused to cough it up and spat at me when I asked for an extra quarter to cover the interest. That's what's wrong with the world, Father. These people have no respect. I mean zero, zilch, zippo... the big O." His head shifted sideways. "Hello, pretty lady."

That was when she walked in—the most dangerous person at the meeting. Seth's eyes followed her painted-on, faded blue jeans across the room, his own pair becoming tighter with every step she took. Her blonde ponytail swished, from side to side, in time with her curvy hips as if they had practised their movements. Who ever she was, she didn't belong there. That was what made her frightening.

Seth's heart thumped a little stronger, sensing trouble wrapped in a fuzzy pink sweater. Curiosity piqued in his thoughts. He needed to know her story—why she was there and what she had done? Her body language, however, suggested those answers weren't in the public domain. Centuries of people watching had honed his skills. His assessments were rarely wrong. Complete silence, avoidance of contact, and gaze averted to the floor, were the telltale signs of someone who didn't want to share their life experiences, or even a cordial greeting, for that matter.

An undivided interest in the girl meant the three smokers managed to stroll in undetected and were already seated. He glanced from one to another. It was doubtful any of them were mathematicians, but they effectively found a way to keep as safe a distance as possible from the other participants.

Peters picked up a book and jotted down a few notes before nodding. "We have a new member here tonight. Seth, why don't you come join us?"

Seth took stock of the seating options left available one last time. If what the priest said earlier rang true, he was purchasing a six-month timeshare. There would be no moving or trading after the contract was finalized. There were only three people he wanted to keep in his sights. Trust for any of them wasn't about to be given lightly.

Priests always had something to hide. Peters was no different. Making a deal with the devil was easy—hiding the evidence of the bargain—not so much. Marks were always left when the seal was formalized. There were plenty of full-fledged demons with fewer markings. As for what the man traded, or why, Seth had no interest in. That battle wasn't one he planned on involving himself with. He was in and out in six months, no matter what.

Good old Georgie was the potential second problem. Any man who drank excessively was unpredictable at best. It was all about easing pain. That begged to question where the man's agony stemmed from and if religion was the remedy or the cause. Whoever held the strings to a puppet inevitably had full control of it. Desperation was one heck of a motivator.

That left the girl. His heart banged against his chest—a feeling all but lost to his memories. In all his years, he had never experienced any emotion stronger than anger. In fact, he could think of only two that held such a potential: fear and love. He played with a black onyx ring on his middle finger, contemplating the two. Fear made little sense. As an immortal, he had no reason to be terrified of anything. Love, however, was impossible. Love at first sight was laughable at best. It was the fodder used in cheesy romance novels to keep housewives complacent in their own relationships—a fantasy that somehow made everything better.

"How about you share the story of how you came to be a part of our gathering?" Peters suggested. "That will make it easier for us to help you control your emotions."

Control. There was that word again and it was as deadly as murder. "I was involved in a bit of a scuffle at a local bar," he answered, pressing his lips together in a firm line so nothing unintended would slip out.

"You're the guy that clocked Roy," Josh blurted out, chuckling. His eyes lit up in a wild fire blaze. "I heard you got him good, too!"

"Settle down," the priest ordered. "We aren't congratulating Seth for fighting. We are supporting his decision to leave violence in the past."

"How'd you do it?" Josh questioned, ignoring Peters. "Leaving two black eyes on a guy like Roy, it had to be quite the beatdown."

Seth glanced straight ahead. His vision locked onto a pair of sky blue eyes, with just a touch of silver hidden beneath the surface. Never before had he seen something so beautiful masking a perfected sadness. "It was a lucky punch," Seth mumbled. "I just wanted to stay in one piece."

Disappointment raced around the circle, plowing him over. The punch it packed was stronger than anything Roy could have thrown. That marked the end of their first encounter. The fuzzy sweater girl averted her gaze back to the floor. Her hands neatly folded in her lap.

The rest of the evening sparked little discussions about how the week had gone. Each of the group shared their successes and failures, save one. No one uttered a word to her and she offered even less back.

# Chapter Four

Seth tossed his bag containing the supplements he needed for the next few days. It landed on the floor. He threw himself backward on the bed, landing on his back, facing the ceiling, his legs crossed. The burdened springs cursed him in a language all their own. Tossing his weight around was a load they weren't equipped to deal with. The mattress sagged in the middle, not caring that there wasn't anything else for him to do.

For the most part, he lived a modest life. There had been times when riches and comfort were of the utmost importance, but that era quickly faded. It was hard to pack up and move with a million possessions and even harder to disappear when one was on a list of the rich and famous. It was easier to live without a penny. That didn't mean he was broke, though. He still owned the castles and villas. Money had simply lost its lustre in his eyes. Appreciation of the finer things in life was pointless without someone to enjoy them with in immortality.

Seth focused on a small crack in the ceiling. Perception made a mockery out of him. The longer he stared, the thicker the line became, growing from the size of a single strand of fine hair to the thickness of a cooked strand of spaghetti. Of course, it hadn't actually changed at all. His vision had made the adjustment on its behalf. That was one of the few human failings he had retained. He blinked, resetting the picture to begin the process again.

Finding ways to occupy his time had become a problem several decades ago. One can only read every book in existence so many times. He'd tried newer authors, but found many of the perversions the latest generation of mortals were into laughable. He wasn't judging them, so much as relating to them. They both needed to use pain and suffering to bring about a release. Evolution had brought their two species closer than they had ever been before. If the world didn't destroy itself, one day he might even see the two merge into one omnipotent life form. That would be something worth living for.

His mind wandered to a fuzzy pink sweater—yearning to know how she fit into the forming picture—blended into a collage or singled out for a cameo shot? His heart knocked twice. Whatever her role to play was, at the moment, she was the sole reason he was holding things together. A vampire stripped of all emotions was no better than a rabid dog, except deadlier.

The painful twinge from the upper gums of his mouth alerted him of his affliction. He chuckled musing over an instinct he'd buried long ago. Control of one's fangs was the first thing a new vampire learned. Never before had the mere thought of a person had such a strong effect on his psyche. She made him lose control, and even worse, he didn't know why.

He turned his attention back to the crack, a safer object to obsess over. It, after all, could potentially have consequences one day. Should an earthquake strike, that crack was only the beginning of a structural collapse. Fingers rubbed across his chin in contemplation, coming to an abrupt stop. He bolted up into a sitting position.

*Whiskers!* His thumb took a second pass to confirm the findings. His laughter echoed that of children being tickled. It was true! Even if it was only the stubble beginnings, it was whiskers nonetheless. Hands extended before his view, each nail on display. They too were longer. It wasn't a drastic change in terms of what humans experienced, but for a vampire it was rare. A dead man's hair and nails didn't suddenly become longer. It was a scientific fact. Even though those parts were technically made up of dead cells, of which he had plenty, their growth relied on the circulation of blood.

He raced to a broken mirror, hung loosely on the wall. That earthquake could have brought it down too, sending shards in all directions. Seth wasn't concerned with natural disasters anymore, though. There was something much more exciting on his mind. His heart was functioning at a level strong enough to alter his appearance. Anything would have been a welcome change. Sporting a new moustache or beard was pure fantasy for a vampire. There was even a chance, if it lasted long enough, a haircut would be possible.

He turned his head from side to side, admiring strong profile views. Rumour had it there was a lining in every rain cloud made of pure silver. It seemed he'd found it mixed in with the sky blue of a woman's eyes. There was a storm brewing that normally he wouldn't want to be caught in. This time, however, he could already see the pot of gold at the end of the rainbow.

# Chapter Five

Seth inhaled a breath of air, taking his lungs to capacity for the first time in decades. Breathing was a mortal need, one he hadn't enjoyed when he was alive. For his kind, it was considered only part of the act. He had a theory, and if he were right, it would be a huge breakthrough for vampires everywhere. Not that he knew how many there were, if any. Over the years he'd lost track of them. Travelling in packs brought far too much unwanted publicity to light.

His chest rose and fell in time with his steps. With his heart dancing to its own beat, it was the perfect time to see if replenishing oxygen supplies cleansed the blood enough to stimulate faster hair growth. It was a long shot, but plausible. All the parts existed and were capable of functioning. The switch simply needed to be turned on.

He left early for the meeting; not knowing how long walking to the church would take. Hands shoved in his pockets, he kept what others would view as a brisk gait. From his perception, though, he was moving at a snail's pace.

Seth stopped at the pathway leading to his next meeting. A chuckle escaped parted lips. "Great," he complained, "completely dark." Churches weren't supposed to close. It was their duty to be there for one and all seeking spiritual guidance. He hadn't noticed it before, but something wasn't right about this particular house of God. The search for the parish's name became a game of hide-and-seek—one he was loosing. He moved in closer, phone in hand, ready to search the Internet for anything he could find about the would-be place of worship.

"Psst!"

"Who's there? Show yourself!" Seth demanded, spinning around and coming face-to-face with the girl from the smoker trio.

"You got a light?" the girl asked. "I've been waiting here for you to arrive and ran out of matches."

"What for?" Seth retorted, searching his pockets for some matchbook he might have picked up when smoking was still culturally acceptable. He tossed the sole pack containing a half a dozen sticks through the air.

"Thanks," she said, already trying the first. Its spark fizzled. "How old are these things?"

"No clue," Seth replied. "I don't smoke. I'm not even sure how I ended up with them." It was a lie, but the truth was often overrated. "I don't think you were waiting around for me to bring you a light," Seth said. "So are you going to tell me?"

The third match set a blaze just long enough to get what she needed. She inhaled deeply, leaving a line of ash where an orange glow had been. Her eyes closed, hands shaking. There was no doubt she was an addict. "Did you really beat up Roy?"

Seth rubbed the back of his neck. "I'm not very good with names," he admitted.

"Marge," she said, forming an oval ring out of the smoke she exhaled. "Same as the cartoon character, except with normal hair."

"Well, Marge," Seth said, "I'm not sure that is something we should be discussing out here. Why bring this up now?"

"I guess I hoped you were different from the others, seeing as you aren't from around these parts," Marge admitted. "I got my answer. You are just as scared of Roy as the rest of us."

"You lost me," Seth said, his forehead wrinkling. "Who is scared?"

Marge chuckled. "I am. Peters is. You are," she replied. "The whole damn town is. So much so that it's all hush-hush."

Seth shook his head, but didn't have time to respond.

"Don't deny it!" she screamed. "You don't even have the guts to admit you didn't start that fight. It was all Roy."

"How'd you know that?" Seth muttered.

"It always is," Marge explained, a smile wavering, unsure of whether or not it wanted to make an appearance. "Do you know why I am here?"

"No," Seth replied, shaking his head. "I have a feeling you are going to tell me, though." As long as there was any form of government, conspiracy theories were bound to pop up. This had the markings of a doozie.

"It's a small town," Marge started, using the end on her cigarette to light another. She puffed around her words. "Everyone knows I have been recovering from drug use for sometime. The Thompson family and mine have been close for as far back as anyone could remember, so they certainly knew. I was doing well... all things considered. Then, I had a moment of weakness." She shrugged her shoulders. "It happens. I'm human. I went so far as to make a special trip to visit with my old dealer. Who do you think I ran into?"

"Roy," Seth answered.

"Yup," Marge agreed. "He told me to go home. He even said he wouldn't tell anyone he saw me, and I believed him. The next day, I woke up to sirens blaring in my driveway. The sheriff barged in and said he had to arrest me. Before I knew it, I was in front of the judge, hearing about how his son took all these drugs away from me. Roy claimed he was trying to protect me on account of our families being friendly and all." She wiped her nose on her shirt.

"Why?" Seth asked, turning his gaze to meet hers dead on for the first time that night. Black makeup had smudged in some places, and was non-existent in others, forming a warpaint unique to a one-woman clan. Bags sagged under her eyes. If she slept in the past day at all, it hadn't been well.

"Because he was caught with it," Marge blurted out. "In this town, Roy is always in court, but never does any time. We all do instead. I've been working on this theory for a while. There hasn't been anyone to share it with... until now."

"You're kidding!" Seth exclaimed. "The judge gave us both sentences. Roy wasn't let off the hook any more than I was."

"Look around," she said, twirling with her arms out wide. "Do you see Roy here? You both were in the fight. Probably given the same sentence. You agreed to serve your community time. In these parts that's as good as a confession."

"They put the same ankle lock on him," Seth argued. "I saw them. Maybe he's under house arrest or something."

"That was for show," Marge explained, rolling her eyes. "It was to get you to agree to do the time. Don't feel bad. We all fell for it."

"Wait!" Seth exclaimed. "Are you telling me that everyone in this meeting is a victim of Roy and his family?"

"Yeah," Marge answered, lighting another cigarette before flicking the old one away. "And there's nothing we can do about it... especially those of us with the fancy jewellery around our ankles. That's what keeps us in line. No one wants to go kaboom, so we keep our mouths shut and show up to this place when we're told. I don't know if I can handle another two years of this." Her eyes watered.

Seth had no idea why she had picked him for a saviour. He had his own problems to worry about. Making waves didn't fall into any of the plans, especially when he had no idea if she was telling the truth. It was curiosity that demanded he find out, one way or another. The girl had nothing to do with it. His mind wandered to another female from the group and what she could have done to Roy Thompson to end up there.

"Surely in the group, if we all compared notes..." He took a step back from the hand in his face. "Or not..."

"Not," Marge whispered. "There's a piglet on the loose. It squeals real loud anytime someone catches it. That's not healthy."

"It could be me," Seth said, shrugging his shoulders.

"Nah," Marge said, glancing over her shoulder. "You came after the incident that changed things. It couldn't be you. One of the others."

"Incident," Seth repeated. "What incident?"

Marge's knees knocked together. "I've already said too much." She leaned in close to his ear. "Be careful. If something happens to me, they'll come for you next." She headed back up the steps to wait by the door.

"Hey! Do you happen to know the name of this church?" Seth blurted out. "I haven't noticed it anywhere."

"Yeah," Marge replied. "It's Thompson Family Parish. Mrs. Thompson is a bit of a religious fanatic. I told you they controlled everything in this town." Her attitude shifted in a complete one-eighty. "Show them some respect!" She inhaled deeply enough to turn the rest of her cigarette to a pile of ash.

The church doors creaked open.

# Chapter Six

If looks could kill, he would have been sitting in the middle of a massacre and another church scandal. Of course, if Marge was right, it would be cleaned up then buried before news of it got out. The meeting was one of little words, for anyone other than Josh. It was his night to share and that was exactly what he planned to do, in detail. He had only reached the recap of dinner the day after their last gathering.

Seth tuned out the static noise, allowing his own voice to replace everything else. The eerie gut feeling that danger was lurking amongst them hadn't subsided. He took stock of each of the players once again, his eyes coming to rest on a baby blue fuzzy cardigan. He forced his mind back to the previous encounter, looking for a name. No one had mentioned it. In fact, no one spoke to her the entire night. Maybe she couldn't talk or hear.

Seth moved on to the second female in the room, Marge. She sat head down, avoiding everything. Her fingernails alternated between scratching deep into the skin on her arms to being chomped on by chattering teeth. Normally, he'd stay clear of anyone exhibiting that behaviour. Withdrawal was amplified by fear and vice versa. She locked herself in a world all her own and threw away the key to boot. It would take a magician to pull her back out in one piece. He didn't know what his forte was, but it most certainly didn't involve magic tricks.

The question still remained; did they all actually have a run-in with Roy, and was that why they were condemned to the basement of a local church? His instincts told him the equation didn't add up. There was a number missing, and until he figured out what value that was, he couldn't solve the problem.

"Thank you, Josh," the priest said. "It's inspirational seeing how far you have come. We'll take a quick break. I think more than one of us could use a hot cup of coffee." He patted George's shoulder on his way out.

George groaned, uttering a few incomprehensible words that were probably related to not wanting to be woken up. His head bobbed up for a split second before falling back down, chin pressed against his neck. That was the only movement he made until the priest returned. Even then, all the old man mustered was a snort.

"Come on now," Peters said. "A hot coffee will do you some good."

George didn't answer in words, swatting blindly at the cup instead. Each attempt failed to connect by some distance.

"George!" Peters exclaimed. "I can't send you home like this."

That was the first thing Seth and the priest agreed on. George was in a bad way. As far as alcoholics went, he had reached the bottom of the barrel. The fact Peters continued to badger him was mind-boggling. There was no sense trying to reach anyone that far gone.

"I must insist!" Peters bellowed.

The answer from George's lips didn't sound entirely human. Slurred words mixed with low growls amidst chattering teeth. His jaw clamped down, biting his own tongue. A trickle of slobber mixed with a few drops of red slid down his chin.

Peters held his chin up, examining the damage. George's eyes opened, rolling to the back of his head, leaving only bloodshot whites visible.

George inhaled deeply, sitting up straight. "The killer," he said. "I know who did it. They have to catch the killer." He resumed his precious position.

"He needs to sleep it off," Josh suggested. "Maybe we should leave him here. It would be safer than letting him try to walk home. I could stay and watch over him."

"I think you are right, but no need to remain." Peters agreed. "There's no place safer than a house of God. I'll find him some blankets and make him up a bed on the floor. The rest of you are free to go."

Marge bolted for the door, glancing over her shoulder after almost every step. The other two smokers followed her footsteps, needing a nicotine fix to calm shaky nerves. Fuzzy sweater girl made her move next. Seth followed.

"Hey," he called out, a few steps behind.

She came to a dead stop. "What?" she whispered, biting her bottom lip as punishment for allowing even one word to escape.

"We haven't actually met," he replied. "I'm Seth." He held out his hand for a friendly greeting. A goofy smile crossed his lips from the sweet sound of her voice. Peters' church didn't need a choir; this girl had the voices of angels from the clouds hidden within it. There was no other explanation for something as trivial as one word reaching the cold dark heart of a vampire.

She glanced at the offering, without making any attempt to reciprocate. "That's not a good idea," she said. "Stay away from me, please."

"At least tell me your name," Seth complained.

"Jenny," she said. "Now go away before anyone sees us talking."

# Chapter Seven

Jenny's words haunted Seth. There was something going on that went further than anger management classes, and he was the only one who didn't seem to know what. Coincidences were lining up, but they didn't form anything concrete. Secrets were an immortal's demise. It was one thing to go to the grave without ever finding answers; it was another to be plagued throughout eternity. If he didn't find out while he was there, he never would. Time and people would pass, leaving him to go mad, never finding peace of mind.

He strolled back to the church for another round of self-control for dummies. Dawdling in his thoughts a little too much put him there exactly on time and the last to arrive, save for one other. George's seat was noticeably empty. He glanced from one face to another. Each member of the group held their heads in a manner to completely avoid eye contact with the empty chair.

Seth scratched his head. It didn't make any sense not to acknowledge the man's absence. The only one, other than himself, acting as if anything had happened was Marge. She was a bundle of nerves. Her bloodshot eyes and drooping lids screamed for a few minutes of rest. Trembling lips and shaking legs refused to allow it. A several-day buildup of grease bogged down her hair into a stringy mess. She sat sideways, rocking in her chair and humming to herself.

Peters offered a quick smile, before starting the meeting. "Good evening. I see we are all here. It's your day, Marge. Tell us how things have been."

Against better judgement, Seth took it upon himself to address the elephant in the room. "Shouldn't we wait? We seem to be missing a person."

"I was hoping to avoid any necessary unpleasantness, but since you have brought it up," Peters replied. "At some point the other evening, George passed away. It seems his heart gave out."

"It simply gave out?!" Josh exclaimed.

"Settle down!" Peters ordered. "These things are known to happen to alcoholics. It's nobody's fault and there is nothing anyone could have done to prevent it."

"When is the service?" Seth questioned.

"Sorry?!" Peters replied.

"The service for George," Seth continued. "I'd like to attend. I am sure you have something planned. By coming to these meetings, he was effectively a part of your congregation, after all. I imagine we'd all like to pay our last respects."

"Of course," Peters agreed, a maniacal smile plastered on his face. "There will be a short service Sunday afternoon after regular Mass. You are all welcome to attend." He glanced around the room. "It appears Marge is in no condition to speak today. If there isn't anything urgent you feel we should discuss, perhaps we should make an early evening of it."

"What about our time?" Seth questioned. Being let go early sounded great, unless it added extra time onto his sentence.

Peters sighed. "Attend the service before George's funeral. That will do in the place of this meeting. Agreed?"

Seth nodded. He was planning on being present anyway. Following one of the two girls had been his plans for the evening. With Josh sitting alone, his face buried in his hands, the agenda changed. The rest of the group, including Peters had vacated. For a priest, Peters wasn't big on support for the grieving. A vampire wasn't exactly the next best thing to offer. He rubbed his neck. Someone to talk to was better than nothing.

"Can I buy you a coffee?" Seth asked.

Josh peered between two fingers, his bloodshot eyes trying to hide from the world. "You want to buy me a coffee?"

"Don't get the wrong idea," Seth said, shrugging his shoulders. "I thought you could use an ear to chat to."

"I guess I could," Josh admitted, his hands falling to his sides. "There's a place round the corner that isn't too bad."

"Lead the way," Seth said, following Josh out the door. Friendship wasn't a luxury vampires took part in. They could have pretty much anything else, other than human companionship. People were born and died, but the undead stood the test of time. It made little sense to form a bond when it was already ending.

Seth pulled the collar of his jacket up around his neck, more out of habit than necessity. It was what a human would do at that time of year, in light of a gusty wind delivering its first message from Old Man Winter. It was going to be a cold one. Of course, it would take an enormous weather shift for him to feel even the slightest temperature change. He shoved his hands into his pants pockets.

"So," Seth said, "you and George were friends for a while, huh?"

"We sure were," Josh replied, all traces of his fake accent vanished. "Best friends since childhood. He hit some hard times at the end."

"Do you mind me asking what happened?" Seth questioned, not wanting to appear as insensitive as he actually was.

"I don't mind you asking," Josh said. "Others might not like it, though."

"Others?" Seth echoed.

"Yeah," Josh said. "This town doesn't like its dirty laundry being dug up and dragged all over town. They'd rather sweep it under the rug, no matter what the consequences."

"I'm not sure I follow," Seth admitted.

"I don't suppose you would," Josh said. "You haven't been in town long enough to know anything about it."

"You have my curiosity piqued," Seth said. "Don't leave me hanging. What happened that required a full-scale cover-up?"

Josh chuckled. "You make it sound like a conspiracy theory."

"Isn't it?" Seth asked.

Josh stopped. His lips puckered in contemplation of which words they were going to allow passage to. "I suppose it could be. It could never be proved, though. I doubt it ever will be now... especially with Georgie dead."

"He was a witness to something?" Seth questioned.

"Ah heck. What have I got to lose but my health?" Josh mumbled. "You grab the coffee for the night, and I'll tell you what I know."

"Sounds like a deal," Seth agreed, holding the coffee shop door open. He strolled over to the counter, side-eyeing his companion choosing a table for their conversation.

# Chapter Eight

Seth slid the first of the two to-go cups across the table, keeping his own in hand. There were few mortal delights he could indulge in when it came to eating. A vampire's system was, simply put, more advanced than the human body could ever hope to be. Although he still had all the organs and parts, only a handful of them were actually needed. That meant he didn't have to bother with using a washroom for doing anything other than washing. It also had a downside, though. What went in his mouth needed to be absorbed. Coffee was basically water and caffeine, two ingredients that could be used. Water was a key ingredient in keeping his flesh from rotting. Stimulants went either straight to his heart or brain, depending on where they were needed most.

"Thanks," Josh said, eyes darting around the room. He'd picked a table at the back of the room—as far away from anyone else as possible. That hadn't been difficult; there was only one other patron in the place and she was at the counter ordering.

"No problem," Seth replied. "So what's the dirty little secret everyone seems to be hiding in this town?"

Josh licked his lips, leaning over the table. His voice lowered. "I can only tell you what Georgie told me when it comes to the actual event. He was the sole witness that I know of. It's a very different side to what the town accepts as truth."

"Maybe we should start with the town's version," Seth suggested.

Josh nodded. "It isn't spoken of around here anymore, either. Both are equally as dangerous to be caught gossiping about."

"Funny," Seth mused, "I already figured that part out. I have no plans to become a problem to anyone. All I want is to do my time and get the heck outta here."

"That's a good plan," Josh agreed. He took in a deep breath. "A number of years ago, there was an accident that rocked the town to it's core. A number of youths in the area were drinking heavily... I suspect drug use was a factor as well. They tore through the town, leaving a path of destruction behind them, before playing a game of chicken in stolen vehicles. All parties were killed in the crash, along with a few bystanders."

"That's terrible," Seth acknowledged, "but not uncommon among teens. I've heard that very story a number of times before."

"Yes," Josh agreed, "but what happened after isn't. Two of the deceased were Roy's siblings. His mother took the loss extremely hard, blaming everyone and everything for their deaths. In her mind, they were innocent souls who were at the wrong place at the wrong time."

"That wasn't the case?" Seth questioned.

"That's where Georgie's story differed," Josh replied, his eyes shifting from side to side. "He insisted he saw the Thompson twins in one of the cars and Roy in the other. They were the instigators in it all. He even tried to stop them, but ended up with a lump on his head for the efforts."

"So their family covered it up," Seth said, rubbing his stubble. "And George was silenced by the judge. I take it that's how he ended up in the priest's charge?"

"No," Josh replied, his mouth holding the form of an O for a few moments. "Peters wasn't around yet. Georgie was silenced, though. Mrs. Thompson had a bit of breakdown. The judge wasn't going to let anything make it worse. She'd lost two kids and if the law found Roy responsible, that would have made all three."

Seth took a sip of his coffee. It had cooled considerably since they first arrived, leaving him to wonder if he should offer a grab a new round. "So Georgie kept his mouth shut and Roy got off?"

"Georgie always liked his drink," Josh admitted. "The judge labelled him an alcoholic and said his testimony wasn't admissible. He lost everything: his family, his job, his life. That's when the heavy drinking started. I was the only friend that stuck by him to the end." A gleam in his eye threatened to form tears.

"How did Peters come into the mess?" Seth asked, changing the topic slightly. "And the church's name?"

Josh waggled one finger in the air. "Mrs. Thompson's condition looked as if it were taking a turn for the worse. She turned to her faith in God for explanations and declared a war on the evil infecting the town. Her preaching touched the hearts of anyone who had lost a loved one and needed someone or something to blame. Her found-again-faith led to a sabbatical.

No one thought anything of it at the time. It was at the same camp many of the churches in the area sent youths for a couple of weeks every summer."

"Faith isn't a bad thing for a human to have," Seth suggested. "Finding solace in a god is a way to cope with grief for many."

"You don't understand how extreme the situation was," Josh argued. "With her husband not wanting to set her off further, good people were sent to jail. He made sure Roy did no wrong to protect her."

"Did she find any relief on this sabbatical?" Seth questioned, arching one brow.

Josh leaned further across the table. "She came back worse and with the good priest in tow. That was when things got really bad. It became her mission to unify the town under one religion. All the other churches were closed. Peters became the sole guidance in faith."

"Surely there are other religions in town," Seth argued. "Not everyone believes in the same gods, after all."

"Not a one," Josh said, leaning back for the first time since they arrived. He let out a heavy sigh. "That's when the good judge came up with the idea of their own type of reform."

"The classes," Seth mumbled. "Everyone there has been accused of doing something wrong. Are we the only offenders in town?"

Josh chuckled. "Nah," he said. "We are the only ones who were dumb enough to get messed up with Roy, though. Anyone who shines a light poorly on the boy gets an ankle wrap and time in that room."

"What did you do?" Seth questioned.

Josh's leg thumped on the table. "Nothing," he admitted. "I don't have the bomb treatment. I attended as a volunteer. It stroked the good priest's ego and he let me join. I faked being a bit psychotic to keep an eye on Georgie."

"You did a good job," Seth said, chuckling. "I thought you were the only one who needed to be there. What now? Are you planning on going back?"

"I don't know," Josh admitted. "It would look odd if I simply quit. I'll probably see what happens after the service Sunday."

"What about Jenny?" Seth asked.

Josh's gaze darted to meet Seth's. "Jenny," he said, his hand rubbing through what was left of his black hair. "Don't waste any time on that one. That girl is a death sentence."

"Why?" Seth asked. "What did she do to get into Peters' room?"

Josh eyed the room again, his slightly open mouth showing a wagging tongue, unsure if it should form words or not. In a motion that might have gone undetected under normal circumstances, his head nodded. Perspiration beaded on his forehead. Something was up.

"Well look who we have here," Peters said, approaching the table. "It's good to see you with a new friend, Josh."

"I thought I would lend an ear," Seth said. "It can be hard to lose a close friend."

"Indeed," Peters replied. "And have you found talking things through to be of help? Perhaps you would like to tell me your stories as well?"

"Thanks, Father," Josh blurted out. "I think I'm all talked out." He glanced at his watch. "Is it that late already? I'll be taking my leave. I'll see you both at church on Sunday." Without muttering an actual goodbye, he scurried off.

"Perhaps you'd like to join me?" Seth offered. "I am happy to buy you a coffee."

"Thank you," Peters replied, a grin forming in the corners of his mouth, "but I don't drink the stuff. I'm surprised to see you do. I may have had you pegged wrong. I'll see you on Sunday." He waved over his head as he exited the cafe.

Seth glanced at his coffee cup, then back at the door. Peters left without buying a thing, so why was he there in the first place?

# Chapter Nine

Someone forgot to tell the sky it was daytime. A sheet of grey loomed over the town, threatening a good soaking. It was holding off for the moment, perhaps waiting for the funeral service to shed its tears. Seth couldn't complain, though. It made things easier for him in the long run. Daytime wasn't a vampire's time. They were creatures of the night for a reason. It wasn't what people thought, either. He wouldn't turn to ash or burn in the sun. Direct light did, however, have an adverse effect on his skin. In essence it was the one thing that aged him physically. The damage prolonged exposure caused could take decades to repair. On a dismal day, with plenty of sunscreen and a full suit, it hardly made a difference.

Seth glanced around, feeling the icy grip of death waiting nearby. A nagging feeling told him the Reaper's services weren't yet needed. That wasn't the only distraction, though. He'd never seen a traffic jam in the small town before. This one was a doozie. Horns honked and words flew out open windows. Obscene finger gestures rounded it all off. It was hard to tell these were God-loving people heading to and from their Sunday service.

The church sat a hop, skip, and a jump away. All Seth had to do was cross the road. Instead he stood staring. He wasn't about to try his luck until he could literally look both ways and see nothing before crossing. It also gave him an opportunity to watch the congregation forming, although most of the crowd he hadn't seen before.

Jenny was the first recognizable face to catch his eye. Her blonde hair flowed gracefully in the breeze. Seth's nostrils flared, honing in on her natural scent. Pain in his jaw stopped his admiration. The vampire in him craved her more than anything he had experienced before. Even with the warning, he couldn't move his gaze.

"Hi," Josh said, standing beside him. "Crazy drivers, huh?"

Seth barely nodded, locked in his own personal trance.

"You need to leave Jenny alone. She is Roy's girlfriend," Josh spat out.

"What?!" Seth exclaimed. "That's absurd. Does she have to take anger management classes to date the guy?"

"Shh." Josh held a finger to puckered lips. "It's more because she doesn't want to date him than anything else. I only know the rumours, but apparently she dumped him. He wouldn't accept that. His mother never would have either." He nodded to the Thompson trio coming down the sidewalk. "Here they come."

"I don't get it," Seth said. "If she hasn't done anything wrong, then how is she stuck in the classes?"

"Firstly, her family is good friends with the Thompsons," Josh explained. "Roy is the jealous type. I mean really jealous. He picked fights for even a casual look in her direction. It wasn't something that could be continuously covered up... albeit they tried. That's when she broke things off, but Roy wouldn't let her go. He stalked her, threatened her, and ultimately attacked her."

"The town looked the other way, I'm guessing," Seth said.

"Not exactly. Mrs. Thompson ultimately found out," Josh replied "Her preaching started up in full force... Jenny's soul was burdened by the devil. Pure evil was using her to try to infiltrate the faith the town had built, by putting a spell on her son."

"She blamed Jenny?" Seth asked, one nostril lifted higher than the other. "That's insane."

"That's the Thompsons," Josh said. "He still stalks her, too. I've seen him drive by before, and after classes, too many times to count. If Peters ever clears her, it's likely she'll be forced into marriage. That's why she doesn't have a device on her ankle. She'll keep going to stay away from Roy."

"That's terrible," Seth said.

"It is, but if you want to get out of town with only a short sentence, you best stay clear of Jenny," Josh suggested. "Looks like we can cross."

Seth shook his head, following him to the other side of the road. The two paused, waiting for the Thompson family to pass through the front doors before heading in themselves. There was no need for any chance confrontations in front of the whole congregation.

Inside, an organ played songs written long before. Peters offered a formal greeting to each member. Unfortunately, that resulted in a gathering around the priest. Not everyone was satisfied with a simple hello and welcome.

Seth considered bypassing the whole process, but wasn't sure if their customs allowed it. The more he heard about the church, the less recognizable the religion was. He hung back behind Josh, hoping not to be noticed by Roy or his father.

"Jenny," Mrs. Thompson bellowed. All idle chatter stopped. "Father, tell me. How has she been doing? Is there any progress?"

Peters nodded. "There would be if Jenny would open up to us a bit more," he admitted. "I'm sure things will improve soon."

"That's good news," Mrs. Thompson said.

"Why don't you sit with me, Jenny?" Roy blurted out. "I always save you a place at my side. It'll be like old times."

Jenny bit her lip. A flush came over her face. "Thank you, but today is a group attendance. I think I should stay with the others, especially with the service afterward."

"Service?" Mrs. Thompson repeated, her voice lifting. "What service?"

"It was an unfortunate incident," Peters replied. "I didn't want to upset anyone with the details. One of the group passed away quite suddenly... a heart issue. We are holding a little funeral for him after the main service today."

"I see," Mrs. Thompson replied. "I trust it won't affect things for the rest of us."

"Of course not," Peters replied. The two exchanged equally unnerving grins. "Ah, Seth. I'm happy to see you here. I had you pegged as a child of the night. I guess I was wrong."

Seth offered a meek smile, forgoing the handshake as he passed by.

# Chapter Ten

If anyone had bothered to make a video of Marge over the past few days, they would have documented her decline from a normal social deviant to an incoherent bundle of rattled nerves. As it was, no one did, nor did they seem to notice her dire situation. She sat, scrunched as close to the corner of the back pew as possible, rocking back and forth in slow motion. Stringy dark hair fell down over her face, hiding bits and pieces from view. The bags under her eyes had their own luggage, black makeup smudged over both. It wasn't the only place, though. A smear of a cross had been made in the centre of her forehead— an odd addition to Marge's usual look.

Even with Seth's extraordinary hearing, he couldn't make out the mumbling noises the girl spewed out under her breath. The inner conversation was meant only for one: herself.

Occasionally, she sang a few bars of one tune or another. He had heard of those able to pick up on radio wavelengths sent from otherworldly sources, but never seen a case up close and personal. Marge's behaviour was showing signs that she was possibly one of these elusive supernatural receivers. The human mind was never meant to handle that type of communication.

Jenny clung to the end of the other side of the same pew, her muscles poised for a speedy getaway. Seth squeezed by her, allowing their knees to touch, if only for a moment. The back of his legs hit the mini shelf holding prayer and hymn books. An electrical shock shot through his body. The kaboom of a thumping heart startled even him. Never had he heard it beat so clearly; so loudly. Her eyes darted up to meet his gaze—she heard it, too. The glimmer in her expression wasn't one of fear, though. It was soft, calming, understanding. It was love.

Seth scooted across the pew, centring himself between the two women. A hymn book in hand, he flipped through the pages, avoiding contact with either side. A neck stretch, ending in a loud cracking noise, garnered the attention of those seated directly in front. "Sorry," he mumbled, angling his gaze at the ground. One foot played with a kneeling bench. It flipped up and down, eventually refusing to move again. He had only been there a few minutes and already something was broken.

A rush of different emotions flooded through his body. The simple contact exchanged between himself and Jenny had opened up the dam and everything was rushing through. He almost felt human again. That wasn't possible, though. He was without question a vampire. His fangs threatened to emerge as proof of that very fact. His lips pursed together, mouth wiggling to stop their extension.

The service itself was underway, not that he could concentrate on anything being said. The sound of his own heart drowned out all words. She was all he could think about. Lust was an emotion he had experienced before. This was different. It was more. There were other feelings intertwined with it. Seth closed his eyes, trying to bring up a memory of when he last felt such a draw; only her face appeared. He hadn't believed in love at first sight when he was alive—he certainly wasn't going to now that he was dead.

Seth's mind raced over all of the things it could have been. As a vampire, he wasn't susceptible to potions or bites. Another vampire couldn't hypnotize him, nor would they want to try. Attempting such a feat would only render the fool trying insane. He glanced at Marge. It was possible that was what happened to her.

The hymn book landed on the ground. Seth bent over to pick it up, stealing a glimpse at the other side of the aisle. Marge's smoking buddies had several pews to themselves. Apparently, the congregation wanted nothing to do with them. He sat back up, thumb flipping pages again. Josh was missing. George was his best friend, there was no way he would duck out early and miss the services. There had to be another reason why he wasn't sitting in the back.

The priest called for all to stand. That was a chance to look around. After the congregation was asked to sit again, he would have a spit second to scan the room without drawing too much attention to himself.

His foot tapped, as prayer and hymn passed, yet not once did the priest allow them to sit. Although he was for the most part considered tall, he was by no means the largest man in the room. Peeking over top of heads was only going to get him so far. Even on his tiptoes he couldn't find Josh in the crowd. He would have to wait. Patience was a virtue, after all. Too bad vampires weren't the virtuous type.

# Chapter Eleven

The occasional yawn accompanied empty expressions as the congregation filed out in a single line. The regular service was over. Peters ducked out a side exit at the front of the room and was already by the exit doors, wishing each and every soul a wonderful week. The members of the anger management class were the only ones who remained seated—Josh still noticeably absent.

Seth glanced around, wondering for the first time where the body was being kept. For some it might have been a morbid thought, but to the undead, death was a part of living. If George was being stored somewhere, he hoped air conditioning was on in the room. The stench of rotting flesh wasn't a pleasant one.

The last of the churchgoers made their way out. Peters closed the doors behind them, heading back inside, already removing various layers of his priestly uniform.

"Come along then," Peters said. "I didn't want to upset anyone who came here for worship, so I set up another room for George. Follow me."

The group filed out in a single line, following the priest as if they were his dedicated choirboys. Peters rounded the front pew, passing the organ, and straight through the side door. He didn't even bother to hold it open for the person behind him. Jenny managed to catch it before it slammed in her face. The group continued in the same formation down a corridor, passed several rooms including a dinning area, offices, and a full theatrical stage, before coming to a set of stairs heading down.

At the bottom was yet another hallway. This one had doors on either side. Peters stopped, pointing to the first one on the left. "In there," he said.

It could have been hell in all its glory behind that door— every inch filled with fire and brimstone. It wouldn't have mattered. They all filed in obediently. Luckily, it wasn't. In fact, all that was in the room was the coffin, some plastic folding chairs and Josh. At least he wasn't lost anymore.

Seth took another look around, wishing he'd picked up a bunch of flowers. There weren't any floral arrangements or wreaths to be seen. There also wasn't a single picture of George. He took a seat beside Josh.

"I wondered where you got to," Seth whispered. "I was looking for you during the service. Were you in here the whole time?"

"Yeah," Josh replied. "Father Peters had his hands full, so he asked me to ready things back here." He glanced over both shoulders. "I did the best I could."

Seth patted him lightly on the back. "You did great," he said. "George was lucky to have a friend like you."

"Thanks," Josh said. "I've already said my goodbyes. I think I could use some air."

Seth glanced around, his brow wrinkling. "Isn't someone going to say something?" It was too late though, everyone else had already left the room. His hands smacked down on his legs, a sigh releasing at the same time.

Closed coffins were one thing a vampire never trusted. To truly know a loved one was dead and gone, one needed to see the body. Seth glanced around before carefully prying the lid open. He shook his head, a chuckle hiding in his breath. There was no body. That begged to question; where was George? There were only two people who could answer: Josh or Peters.

Backtracking, he headed back up the stairs in the now empty building. Other than his own footsteps, the only sounds were those of the building settling. He'd heard similar before. Someone skimped on building materials. It didn't make a difference for the first half century, but the foundation was weak nonetheless.

If Josh had already flown the coop, at least Peters could answer a few questions. Seth headed to the main offices, finding one door partially open. From a distance he could make out figures and voices. Marge was with the priest. He moved so as not to be noticed.

"Do you admit?" Peters called out. "Do you renounce the evil within you?"

"I am not evil," Marge argued. "Please, Father. I am not a demon. I swear it. I have done nothing wrong."

"I cannot help you, child, until you are ready to accept the truth," Peters said. "Begone from me if you are too weak."

"I need your help, Father," Marge cried. "I can't sleep. I can't eat. I'm frightened. They are going to hurt me."

"I have offered the only help I can give," Peters replied. "What say you, child? Will you take the first step toward the light?"

"I will," Marge agreed, albeit reluctantly.

"Then tonight I shall perform the ceremony," Peters announced. "We'll rid you of your demons, once and for all. There's a room in the basement where you can prepare for nightfall."

Seth took the fastest route out of the building. Whatever Peters was planning, he wanted in on it as an observer.

# Chapter Twelve

The skies rumbled—displeasure danced in the wind. No one beat the Grim Reaper and got away with it. He was the one immortal who always won in the end. The undead were the exception to that rule—a pact made in the beginning of days that was never put in writing. Death didn't deal in ink. Put simply, vampires were allowed to exist, until they didn't anymore.

Seth glanced around. He hadn't felt the same dark presence inside the church. Outside, the Reaper was still there, hiding around one corner or the other. It was odd Death didn't enter; he was as close to a god as an immortal could be. There wasn't a religion or affiliation that held favour over the cold steel of his scythe. No one in town was exempt, nor would they be safe that evening. When the bill came due, it had to be paid. There was no hiding from that. The power necessary to keep the Angel of Death at bay was unfathomable.

Seth pulled his jacket closed. There was no one left out front. He took to the sidewalk, glancing both ways and barely catching sight of the one person he wanted to see more of. Jenny was about to round a corner four blocks down. A car screeched round the turn, cutting off her path. He didn't need exceptional hearing to know the driver blowing off steam was Roy. His voice raised — words slurred — alcohol was involved.

Seth watched helplessly. There wasn't much he could do with a bomb wrapped around his ankle. One word from Papa Bear and kaboom. Still, he found himself heading in that direction. If there was a chance to intervene without anyone knowing, he wasn't above taking it. Of course, no witnesses meant that Roy wasn't making it out alive. He breathed a little easier seeing Jenny side-step Roy's car and continue down the sidewalk.

The black muscle car spun its tires, leaving smoke and skid marks on the road. Roy was back on track and following her at a snail's pace. Every so often the engine revved followed by a brake stand.

"Hey-y, honey," Roy bellowed, hanging out his window. "You are a naughty girl. You changed your phone number on me."

"You broke my phone," Jenny replied. "I had to get a new one."

"I want that number," Roy demanded. "And I want it now!"

Jenny came to a complete stop. "All right. Are you ready?" she asked. "Here goes... Eight – six – seven – five."

Roy snorted, trying to focus on his own phone. "This sounds familiar. Is it similar to your old one?"

"Yup, it sure is," Jenny lied. "Three – O – Nine."

"Got it!" Roy announced.

"Great you can call it for a good time," Jenny said, a smirk spanning her entire face.

Seth chuckled. That woman had a sense of humour and he liked it. It was bound to get her in trouble if what Josh told him about the two was true. Still the smile wasn't about to leave his face for a long time.

A line of cars honked at the well-below limit speed. Roy offered a single finger as his initial response, but pulled over to the side to allow the traffic to pass. That gave Jenny the chance she needed. Her speed picked up, allowing her to put a block between herself and the muscle car before ducking into a store. It was hardly a victory, though. Roy pulled up in a parking spot across the street. He stood in front of the driver's side door, arms crossed over his chest, waiting.

With his jean cuff covering the mandatory anklet and his jacket collar pulled up to hide his face, Seth headed into the convenience store. It was risky, but Roy was intoxicated and preoccupied. Finding a way to get both of them out of there unnoticed wasn't going to be easy, though.

"Hey," Seth said, walking by Jenny.

She spun around. "Are you following me?"

"Nope," Seth lied, grabbing a cold bottle of water from the back fridge. "I wanted a drink. That's not a crime."

"And you just happened to stop at the store I'm in?" Jenny asked, raising her brows. "A mere coincidence."

Seth pursed his lips together, making a throaty chuckle. "You mean the store you are hiding from your ex in, don't you? I'm not one to judge, but seems like you need a way out."

"And I suppose you know of one?" Jenny snapped.

"As a matter of fact, I do," Seth answered, heading to the cash to pay for the water.

"How?" Jenny asked, trying to remain hidden from the front window.

"How much is this?" Seth asked. He grabbed the bottle Jenny was holding. "And this, too, please."

The store owner eyed the couple up and down. "Four dollars," he said.

"Would it be all right if she used the bathroom?" Seth asked. "She really needs to go and is a bit shy to ask herself."

"Yeah," the store owner replied. "It's in the back. How do you two know each other?"

"Church," Seth replied. "We met at church. I'm just trying to be neighbourly." The man nodded he was satisfied with the response.

"It's through there," Seth said, directing Jenny to the back door. His voice lowered to a whisper, "Go out the back door. I'll meet you in the alley. It's the safest exit you can make with Roy lurking in the other direction."

"You can't be serious," Jenny complained. "It's not safe for a girl in an alley after dark. What about the buddy system? Come with me."

"I can't," Seth explained. "If the shopkeeper thinks something is up, he'll call in the law. That would be a huge mess. It'll only be for a couple of minutes, I promise. I'm going out the front and heading around the building to meet you. Then I'll take you home. Of course, if you'd rather take your chances with Roy out front."

"No!" Jenny exclaimed.

"Then thank me for my help in a loud voice and skedaddle," Seth said.

"Thank you," Jenny called out. "I really appreciate your help."

Seth waved his hand over his head. "See you next Sunday. Have a good week." The store owner glanced up from his magazine, then back down. He'd been fooled. All that was left was to sneak by Roy one more time.

# Chapter Thirteen

Jenny crossed her arms, hands rubbing them from shoulder to elbow. The temperature had dropped a few degrees—at least it felt like it had. Grey skies turned black. Night crept in while she was dawdling in the store.

Garbage bags rustled in a nearby container. Jenny was no expert when it came to dumpster-diving, but she had watched enough late-night crime shows to consider a murderer, or a rabid rat or raccoon the cause. Neither were things a small-town girl should have to experience. Then again, neither was what Roy had done to her. A shiver left goosebumps on her skin. The very thought of him made her nauseous. The past couldn't be changed, but it damn well wasn't going to repeat itself. Not if she had any chance of stopping it.

Things in town had been uncomfortable since the incident. Every glance judged her. Every laugh mocked her. Every man thought she was easy prey. There was little she could do about it, though. In the end, she had nowhere to go: no money, and no support from her family or anyone else, for that matter. That meant she was stuck. For the most part, keeping her head down and going to Father Peters' classes was enough to keep Roy at bay. When he was drunk, however, it was a whole other story. It wasn't the first time she had narrowly escaped his grasp. If she stayed in town, it wouldn't be the last either.

*Men!* Jenny sighed. He was late. The truth was Seth was the first male she'd trusted since that night. He was also the first man she'd been attracted to as well. She huffed at her taste in the opposite sex. They all let her down and hurt her in the end. Roy for what he did to her. Her father for not believing her story. Seth for leaving her stranded in an alley with rabid wild animals and murderers. Her eyes watered, tears threatening to fall. Instead the skies wept for her.

"Great," Jenny complained. "Just what I needed, an impromptu shower in my Sunday best."

"Then we better get out of rain," Seth suggested. "Lead the way to your place. I'll escort you to the door."

"I can't go there," Jenny blurted out. "It's the first place Roy will go to find me. He has a key, too."

"Did you consider it might be a good idea to change the locks?" Seth suggested.

"I have," Jenny barked, "numerous times. Roy goes to my landlord and insists on a copy every time."

"There are laws against that sort of thing," Seth said.

"Not here there aren't," Jenny argued. "What Roy wants, Roy gets. I happen to be the number one toy on that list."

"Leave," Seth said. "Pack up and move. Roy won't have any power outside of this town. I doubt he'd give up what he has to follow you."

"And go where? Do what?" Jenny questioned. "Trust me, I've been over all the possibilities a thousand times in my mind. I'm stuck right here."

"Okay," Seth said. The skies opened up, rain pelting down in sheets. "We'll make a run for my place. Hopefully, we won't be too drenched when we get there."

Jenny nodded, pulling her sweater over her head. It was useless; the wool was already soaked through. All she managed to do was obscure her vision further.

Seth grabbed her arm, saving her from going for a tumble in the pool of water that had formed in a pothole.

"Thanks," Jenny muttered.

"Keep moving," Seth ordered, without releasing his grip on her arm. He pulled her along with him to the front steps of his building. He shook his head, water spraying from his hair.

Jenny chuckled, adding a sprinkling of her own. "I don't think it is going to make much of difference."

Seth returned her smile. "Probably not, but it worth a try. I have some towels upstairs. We'll dry off as best we can. Then we need to have a chat."

"A chat?" Jenny echoed, forming a question with her voice. "About what?"

"Something isn't right about this town," Seth said. "I want to know what's going on before I get any further involved. We can start with what happened to George's body."

"What do you mean?" Jenny asked. "We saw the casket earlier."

"Yeah," Seth agreed, "but it was empty."

# Chapter Fourteen

Jenny stood just inside the front door, shivering. Her eyes wandered around the room. There wasn't much to keep them occupied. "Not big on possessions, huh?"

"I have what I need," Seth replied, handing her a robe and a towel. "I move around a lot. Not keeping stuff makes it easier."

"Why?" Jenny questioned. Her fingers ran over the terry cloth bathrobe she'd been handed. Putting it on meant taking her other clothes off. She bit her bottom lip, stopping it from trembling. It wasn't only Roy she didn't trust; it was all men. Seth, however, she was finding hard to loathe on the same level.

Seth alternated glances between the robe and her face. "You don't have to, if you don't want to. I thought you might like to dry off a bit." He stripped in the bathroom, leaving his wet clothes in the tub. "I like to see the world; learn new things; meet new people. Let me know if it is safe to come out."

Jenny's dress fell to the floor, the robe on in a flash. "I'm covered," she said. "Do you travel alone..." Her words trailed off.

Seth offered a wink as he passed her, a towel wrapped around his midsection. "Sorry I should have taken some clothes with me." He disappeared back into the bathroom. "I am single, if that's what you are asking."

"No," Jenny protested. "I was just curious. It seems like a lonely life is all. Were those angel wings on your back?"

"You like them?" Seth questioned.

"They are stunning," Jenny replied. "Is there a story behind them?"

"More of an inside joke," Seth admitted. "While I am enjoying our conversation, I am afraid we have more important matters to discuss."

Jenny flopped on the bed. "I don't know anything," she whined. "I assumed George's body was in the casket. I certainly wasn't going to open it to double-check. That fact you did is a bit concerning."

"I don't take people at their word," Seth said.

"Including me?" Jenny asked.

Seth paused. "You might be the exception. What can you tell me about the others?"

Jenny sat back up, shrugging her shoulders. "I told you I don't know anything. After the Thompson twins passed away, the town changed. Grieving can do that. I didn't think anything of it at the time."

"And now?" Seth asked.

"I don't know what to think," Jenny admitted. "Your questions are rather frightening, but for some reason when I'm with you, I don't feel afraid."

"What about Roy?" Seth asked. "Did he change?"

"Roy was always a dick," Jenny replied. "Nothing changed there." Her blue eyes twinkled, glancing over the all-black attire he had chosen.

"And Peters?" Seth continued, clearing his throat.

"Is a priest," Jenny answered. "You know as much about him as I do. He came to take over the town's needs where others failed. Is he doing it? Not really. He's on par with the ones before him, I suppose."

"That doesn't really help," Seth admitted. "I'm going to head back to the church. I heard Peters say there was some type of ceremony going on tonight."

"Wait!" Jenny exclaimed, rushing up to him. She tossed her arms around his neck, planting a kiss on his lips.

Seth's heart thumped in rhythm with hers. "Why did you do that?"

"I was afraid I might not get another chance," Jenny admitted. "I didn't want to wonder what it would be like for the rest of my life."

"That's not going to happen," Seth said. He leaned in closer, his mouth on hers. Passion flared between them. "I'm coming back, I promise."

Jenny's stomach growled.

"In a few minutes with some food," Seth said, chuckling. "Anything in particular you would like?"

# Chapter Fifteen

Jenny jumped the moment the door closed. Her curiosity compelled her to find out more about her stranger. He was different from other men, yet somehow the same. If secrets were lurking in the hole he called a home, she was going to find them.

The closet was the obvious first choice. Her hands fumbled over a half dozen shirts and an equal number of jackets, checking every pocket. Save for an old pack of matches, the search came up empty. The matchbook flipped from front to back in her hand several times. The name on the front wasn't one she recognized. Phone in hand, she swiped the blank screen, before inputting her code. The Internet would tell her what she needed to know. The words *Silver Rail* appeared in the search bar. Her thumb pressed down. Instantly, she had a list of possible answers. Matching the address and location, she found the place.

Her brows furrowed, mouth twitching. The answer didn't make any sense. She flipped the matchbook over again; making sure all the information was accurate. It was. The Silver Rail was a nightclub that opened in the 1940s and had shut down some time in the early 1970s, before she was even born. Seth couldn't have been more than five years older than her.

Time was too short to waste on more questions. The matchbook landed on the bed. The dresser was the next place to rummage through. Her fingers brushed over the wooden surface, coming to rest on a notebook and pen. While Seth didn't seem like the type to keep a diary, it was intriguing nonetheless. Jenny snatched to book up, flipping from page to page, scanning the words delicately written within. A few steps backward found her falling on the bed. Her attention never faltered from the story being told.

Jenny's eyes widened, taking in as many details as she could before flipping the page to start again. There was too much for her to finish before Seth returned with the food. Skipping details, she extracted what appeared to be the important parts.

One: Seth was a vampire. Two: Vampires weren't the same as movies portrayed, although there were some similarities. Three: Vampires weren't affected by religion as she had thought. They could even practice as a devout follower or become part of the clergy. Four: It was easier to move about at night, but they could walk in the day if the need arose. Five: They didn't need to feed on blood. Six: Vampires would do anything to feel their hearts beat again. Seven: He could turn her, but it wasn't from a bite.

The door opened. Jenny tossed the book behind her back, but it was too late. Seth had already seen what she was up to.

# Chapter Sixteen

"What are you doing?" Seth asked, dropping a paper bag containing a variety of different fast foods.

"I-I," Jenny stuttered.

Seth snatched the journal from behind her. "Did you read this?" His eyes fell on the matchbook. "Were you searching my room?"

"I'm sorry," Jenny cried, bursting out in tears. "I don't have the best track record with men. After what Roy did..."

"I'm not Roy," Seth blurted out.

"I know that, but I needed to know who you are," Jenny replied.

"And why is that?" Seth asked, feeling a pulse rise with his temper. He rubbed his upper lip, massaging his gums where fangs were popping through. They were tired of being denied.

"Because," Jenny whispered, "I'm falling in love with you. I know it sounds strange. We barely know each other."

Seth felt his temper subside, but his heart rate increased. He pulled her into a tight hug, feeling the warmth of her body against his own. Rule number one was to never tell any human what he was. Any vampire who broke that rule ended up on the wrong end of a stake. The truth was a wooden stake through the heart would kill just about anyone. Of course, if it was pulled out again, they likely came back. Decapitation and fire were the only ways to ensure a vampire stayed down.

"You can trust me," Jenny whispered, her tears but a memory. "I can feel your heart beat. That's because of me, isn't it?"

"Jenny..."

"It's okay," Jenny interrupted. "I'm not afraid."

"Jenny..."

"I want to leave with you," Jenny blurted out. "You could change me." She offered her neck to him.

"Jenny," Seth yelled, pulling away from her. He was almost ready to confess everything, but changing her was the last thing he wanted to do. A vampire's life was hard and cold. "I'm not sure what you think you know, but what I wrote in that journal is fiction."

"I don't believe you," Jenny said, shaking her head. "You are trying to protect me. I don't need it, though. As long as we are together, our hearts will beat."

"Jenny, I'm sorry," Seth said. "I'm writing a book. There are no such things as vampires. If there were, I wouldn't want to be one. I'm going to check things out at the church. Eat something. I'll be back in a while."

Before he could turn, he felt cold steel breaking the skin on his back. His hand reached over his shoulder, but couldn't pull the blade out.

"You dirty pig," Roy screamed, running at him.

Seth sidestepped the tackle, watching his opponent fall to the ground. All his years of practice meant he knew exactly how to keep Roy down without doing any permanent damage.

"How did he know you were here?" Seth asked, staring at the unconscious body. He grabbed some rope from a drawer to bind Roy's hands.

"I don't know," Jenny replied. "He must have figured it out."

"How?" Seth questioned. "He never saw us together."

"Maybe he saw you go into the store," Jenny suggested. "Or maybe he saw us in the alley and followed us here."

"It took too long for him to show up," Seth said, still fighting to reach the knife lodged in his back. "Would you mind?"

"You want me to pull it out?" Jenny squealed.

"Yeah, that would be better than walking around with it sticking out," Seth replied. "Just close your eyes and pull."

Jenny's hand shook as it grasped the smooth handle. She bit her lip, holding her breath as she yanked it out.

"Thanks," Seth said.

"It didn't kill you," Jenny muttered. "You are a vampire."

"I'm very lucky," Seth argued. "He missed hitting any major organs."

"I'm going to wash up," Jenny said, disappearing into the bathroom. "I want to go to fetch some clothes."

"It's too dangerous," Seth complained. "You should stay here."

"It isn't safe here, either," Jenny said. "I only live a few blocks away. I'd feel better not having a choice between soaking wet or bathrobe."

"I know how far away you live," Seth answered.

"How?" Jenny asked, turning off the faucet.

"I followed you home after class once," Seth admitted.

"That's stalking," Jenny complained.

"I don't know why I did it," Seth said. "I guess I was curious. You are different from other women I have met."

"So you are finally admitting you love me too?" Jenny asked, her back flat against the bathroom door.

"I don't know what it is," Seth admitted. "Maybe it is love."

A smile crept over Jenny's lips, a wildfire igniting in her eyes. "But you want to find out, right?"

"Yeah," Seth agreed. "I guess I do. For now, though, I have to go back to the church. Neither of us is safe until I figure out how to get rid of the ankle jewellery the police gave me. Wait here." He grabbed a few tools and a roll of duct tape. It was better to be prepared for anything—it was likely to happen.

Jenny heard the door shut. Her smile transformed into a knowing grin. The knife held her reflection and his blood. Her tongue extended, cleaning it of all traces of red.

# Chapter Seventeen

A cricket chirping its song in the rose bushes was the only sign of life outside the church. No light shone through the stained-glass windows. At night they each portrayed a much different scene. Pictures of salvation and goodness were corrupted by darkness. Shadows of evil lurked in the background in ways that affected even a vampire.

Seth glanced around, sticking close to the bushes. He skittered the perimeter of the building, looking for a way in, other than the front doors. There was one in the back, meant to lead out to the back garden on a summer's day for afternoon refreshments. Although, the garden was well kept, the entrance hadn't been used for some time. Peters had said the church's doors never locked, and stayed true to his word. It squeaked open without much force.

Seth's eyesight adjusted to a new level of darkness. The inside was pitch-black. For a vampire it wasn't a problem, but humans would need something with which to light their way. In the old days, there would have been a torch waiting to be lit mounted to the wall. An empty bracket remained, mocking would-be trespassers.

Unwelcome visitors had the last laugh, though. Those without night vision had other means. Modern technology had them covered. Every cell phone came equipped with its own flashlight built in. There was no way to tell from that alone if anyone had come or gone from that route. A lack of cobwebs suggested it had been used by someone.

Seth followed the corridor to an entrance beside the kitchen. If there was a ceremony going on, it wasn't anywhere close by. After checking each of the rooms, he headed to the staircase. There was no rush to leap down. On the contrary, he took each step as if it were on the verge of collapse, gingerly testing the surface before making a move. If someone was lurking below, he wasn't about to announce his presence.

He paused with only a few steps left. Voices drifted to his ears. These weren't the sweet sounds of angels. It was something else, altogether.

"Put you trust in me," Peters demanded, holding up a hammer. He moved toward her ankle, poised to strike the contraption bound to her.

Marge screamed. "Wait! We'll both die." She crouched into a ball.

Peters ignored her plea, smashing the locks in one blow. Nothing happened. The priest waited for Marge to glance up before laughing.

"It was never real," Marge muttered. "It was all a lie."

"Not entirely," Peters argued. "The tracker works, most of the time. The next version will be much more reliable. The bomb was a lie, though. That's what kept you in line. We can't have your kind running about infecting the town, now can we?"

"What are you going to do to me?" Marge asked, her voice shaking.

"We are going to save you, my dear." Peters answered. "Once you are cleansed, life will be much better. It is the will of God that all evil be banished from this world. To prepare, you will pray until the midnight hour. Then we will begin."

Seth glanced at his watch. There were still a few hours before midnight. Footsteps warned him Peters was approaching. He backtracked to the rear entrance. A screwdriver banged against the contraption on his ankle. He'd been a fool to think it was real. A range of emotions came over him: anger for being so stupid, pity for Marge, concern for Jenny, hate for the priest running a sideshow on God's dime. None of it should have mattered to him. Vampires were primal beings. Rage was all he needed. Something in him was changing, but why?

All he could think of was Jenny. Perhaps it was love and not just the lust of a monster for a beautiful woman. His mind believed it. His heart concurred. His gut, however, had a different view of things.

Out of the corner of his eye, a shadow caught his attention. Seth was no longer alone in the garden. Whoever else was there would have seen the anklet lying in pieces around his foot. They had to be silenced if he was to have any hope of an escape from that place. A pain jabbed at his chest. It wasn't the same as the knife in his back. This agony came from within. A shadow passed by once again. More than just one person was hiding in the bushes. He needed a plan.

Killing them wasn't the answer. They most likely had a few answers to his questions. He'd tie them up until he was safely away then call someone with their location.

If there was one thing a vampire wasn't, it was prey. Whoever lurked in the shadows was in for a big surprise. They circled Seth, planning to hit from opposite directions. The one on the right was a smidge slower. He sidestepped the left attack, taking down the figure to the right first. It was a textbook play, at least for the supernatural. Humans always liked their buddy system. If only someone had taught them there never was safety in numbers when it came to the paranormal.

Seth snickered. He heard the second attack coming for yards away. A simple hip attack, followed by a sleeper hold did the trick. All he had to figure out now was what to do with them.

# Chapter Eighteen

The best part about church grounds was that they had numerous places, tucked away in one corner or another, meant exclusively for spiritual reflection. Seth sat on the park bench, doing exactly that. The past weeks had changed him in ways he didn't yet fully understand—in ways that shouldn't have been possible. Six months ago, faced with the same scenario, he would have been long gone the moment the anklet hit the ground. There was no rhyme or reason to why he was choosing to stick around. He had no business caring about lives of the people in that town nor did he need answers.

A groan meant his assailants were waking. Hopefully, what the duo had to tell him would satisfy whatever curiosity his appetite had grown. He glanced at the men, bound in duct tape at the ankles, wrists and holding them together back to back via their torsos.

"Welcome back to the living, George," Seth snickered. "Tell me, why the fake death? What's in it for you?"

George struggled against the bindings. "You wouldn't understand," he snapped. "You are an outsider here."

"Try me," Seth demanded. "If you are thinking about yelling for help, keep in mind, I could snap both of your necks and be long gone before anyone stepped foot outside the church to help you."

"We aren't stupid," Josh snarled.

"You must think I am," Seth barked back. "The performance you gave was almost perfect. I admit, at first, you had me going."

"So what gave us away?" Josh asked.

"There wasn't a body in the coffin," Seth admitted. "I knew right then something else was going on. What I don't know is how much of what you told me is fabricated and how much is the truth. What's really going on here?"

The men slouched back against each other, giving up on struggling. Clouds parted, allowing the light of the full moon to shine down, illuminating the faces of two who were not yet completely defeated. Seth chuckled under his breath.

"We can do this two ways," Seth suggested. "I can kill you and keep snooping about, or you can tell me what I need to know."

"There is nothing you can do," George spit out. "You should get out of town while you still can."

"What is Peters up to?" Seth questioned, tossing a blade in the air. It twirled several times before coming back down. He caught it by the handle every time.

"That part is true," Josh said. "He came here to rid the town of evil at the request of Mrs. Thompson."

"Who is he really?" Seth prodded.

"I don't know," Josh admitted.

"I overheard him use the name Macabray once," George added, "but I have no idea what, if anything, that means."

"Macabray," Seth repeated in barely a mumble.

"You have heard that word before," Josh said, straining for a glimpse at his captor's face. He was as curious about the priest as Seth himself.

"I have," Seth admitted, "but it is a bit hard to swallow that you would have an angel cast out of heaven leading the congregation at this church."

"A fallen angel?" George's voice raised a few octaves. "As in Satan? Here?"

"Not exactly," Seth replied. "The Macabray were said to be six of God's finest angels. They followed God's law to the T, destroying evil and casting out those who committed even the slightest of offences. Among angels and demons it is well known those closest to their god received the greatest gifts—the strongest powers. The six siblings expected rewards for their actions. Those rewards never came, though. The Macabray lacked one thing all angels needed: compassion. To learn it, they were sent to live as flesh and blood among the mortals. Only once they proved they understood God's laws could they return."

"So they aren't, technically, evil," George commented. "They are still doing God's bidding, just in a different way."

"That was over a century ago," Seth argued. "They have learned nothing from their time here, or they would have been recalled to the pearly gates. In fact, from what I have heard, they went in the opposite direction. The Macabray are thought to walk the earth in search of those who are most evil, taking their lives in the name of God. The Inquisition, the holy wars, the witch trials are only a few examples. Innocent people accused of crimes for the sake of running a tally great enough to win praise."

"Ridding the world of evil is hardly a bad thing," Josh argued.

"Is your God not a forgiving God?" Seth questioned. "Is it not true that anyone can be absolved of their sins?"

"As a mere human, I don't have the answer to that," Josh replied.

"Maybe you should figure it out," Seth blurted out. "Is he going to murder Marge tonight?" Even the sole cricket was silenced by his tone. "Tell me."

"The list is longer than one," George admitted. "Three will be judged this evening. None will survive the night."

"That's murder," Seth said, "not salvation."

"Perhaps," Josh replied, "but it isn't Peters or the Thompson family pulling the strings."

"What are you saying?" Seth asked. "Spit it out!"

"Jenny," Josh whispered, a chuckle forming on the end her name. A light breeze carried it on its wings, smacking Seth across the face. "From your silence, I can tell she has already taken control of your mind, body, and soul."

"Liar!" Seth yelled.

"It's no lie," Josh argued, laughter filling the space between words. "It was always Jenny. She was the one who set up the race. Two brothers eager to kill each other for her hand. It was her who first met Peters at a youth summer camp. It was her who whispered words into Mrs. Thompson's ear about the sabbatical and suggested bringing back the priest to save the town. She controlled Roy and drove him to drink. In her hands lies enough dirt to ruin half the town's population. Don't think the pretty little thing is above blackmail, either."

"Why should I believe either of you?" Seth questioned, his body shaking.

"Don't take our word for it," George replied. "Ask her yourself. I am sure she has been making a file about you as well."

# Chapter Nineteen

Seth left the two men duct taped to each other and the bench—pieces of the sticky silver over their mouths. Come daybreak, someone would find them. He'd learned all he could from them. Now he needed to find out what, if any of it, was true.

The Macabray name was one only known within supernatural circles. He hadn't given much thought to them over the years, other than staying away from ever coming face-to-face with one. It was doubtful humans could have made that part of the story up. At the same time, the town was small fry for them. They made statements in the name of the Lord that were meant to be noticed. Scare tactics were the devil's tools. Satan wouldn't remain content having competition in his domain for long, though.

The whole situation was a mess he wasn't hired to clean up. A part of him nagged that running for the hills was the only solution. Another, stronger side, still wanted answers. The ball was heading to Jenny's court. He needed to ask her directly.

Death was waiting for Seth outside his apartment. The Reaper hadn't shown his face as of yet, but was lingering nonetheless. The presence was the one thing that could leave goosebumps and stand hairs at attention on a vampire. He raced up the stairs, hoping it wasn't Jenny.

The open door wasn't a good sign, especially since he couldn't sense anything alive inside. Putting off the inevitable wasn't going to change anything. If she was dead, there was nothing he could do. The door creaked further open with the tiniest of pushes.

Seth walked into the middle of a horrific murder scene. It was the work of a human. No self-respecting vampire would leave such a mess. Wasting blood was a sin. He glanced down at the source: Roy. He lay face down in a pool of his own innards, hands still bound behind his back.

The scene didn't match the crime. The room was ransacked from top to bottom, but Roy couldn't have put up a fight. Nothing appeared to be missing, save for three things: Jenny, the murder weapon, and his journal. Smears on the walls and mirrors suggested a psychopath had been finger painting.

Seth stopped at the one clear message: Guilty. Was that meant for him or someone else?

There was even more reason to hit the road running. If anyone saw that mess, he'd be convicted of murder. Someone was framing him, but who? As much as his gut screamed her name, he was sure Jenny could still be as innocent in it all as he was. He needed to find her. If she escaped, there was only one other place she would go, her apartment.

# Chapter Twenty

Security apartments were a joke without a punchline. They displayed all the names and apartments on a list, with buzzer codes for each. It took moments for him to identify Jenny's name. Poof, like that he knew where she lived. All he need was a tenant to go in or out to gain entry into the lobby. There wasn't even a wait. Someone must have read his mind.

Seth caught the door, heading into the building behind a young couple coming home from what appeared to be date night. They exchanged warm smiles before taking different elevators, both being available. He paused staring at the list on floors. His fingers twitched, before pressing down on the one marked PH. That was the first time he realized how little he knew about Jenny. She didn't appear to have a job and yet lived alone in a penthouse. Where did her money come from?

The lift dinged, doors opening to a single front door. That was where some of his other skills came into play. He twisted the doorknob, allowing his extra strength to break the lock, rendering it useless.

Seth's jaw dropped open. The apartment was anything but what he expected. Jenny was supposed to be a suffering soul, ostracized by family and friends. From the looks of things, she was doing little suffering. This wasn't a place to run away from—it was a place people dreamed of living in. From the view of the whole town to every convenience known to man, she had it all. That begged to question; who was paying for it?

"Jenny," Seth called out, not wanting to startle her. "Are you here? It's me Seth. When I saw what happened to Roy, I was worried you might be hurt. I hope you don't mind I let myself in."

It was just as well there was no answer. He had already spotted a few things he wanted to check out, including a safe. Wall safes weren't an entirely new thing. He'd seen them in different styles throughout several ages. One thing they all had in common; they were easy to spot. It was usually a piece of art they were hidden behind: one that either didn't match the owner's tastes or one that held special meaning. A picture of angels hit the mark.

Seth examined all edges before sliding the painting away from the wall. More sophisticated systems would have an alarm attached. This one, however, was as basic as they came. A mere tug pulled the door off its hinges, exposing the treasures within; file folders. They were each labelled with the names of various influential people in the town. He flipped the first one open.

*Dirt sheets!* All the nasty little secrets a person could have were listed with proof in each of those files.

Seth searched his mind for any possible explanation, other than the obvious. It was possible these files were her security and not being used for blackmail in a malicious way. They could have been the reason she hadn't already been forced to marry Roy or wear an anklet.

Seth headed to a desk, booting up the computer. That town had entirely too much influence in finding people guilty without proof. It didn't need him adding to it. The mouse hovered over the files on the drive, clicking on each. There were tax statements in names of people he didn't know, offshore bank accounts, containing decent-sized amounts of money, and pictures.

Seth slouched back as they came up on the screen. Even he had to admit Jenny was no angel. Images of her in various sexual positions with dozens of men stared back at him. Roy was the only one he didn't see, although his father and the sheriff were among the partakers.

It looked more and more as if Josh and George were telling the truth. Jenny ran the town, but he doubted that extended to Peters. He still didn't understand the connection there. The problem was finding out would probably cost him more than he was willing to pay.

He slammed his hand down on the desk, cracking the wood. For better or worse, he was in this until the very end. There was one last place to go. Seth glanced at his watch. It was already almost midnight. The ceremony was about to begin. If he hurried, there was a chance he wouldn't miss it all and perhaps more than one life could be spared from the Macabray. Tonight, for one night only, the roles were reversed. The vampire was destined to be the hero in this storyline—the priest representing all that was unholy in the world. Peters made Satan look like a blessing.

For the first time since before the bar fight with Roy, he allowed his fangs to fully extend, summoning all of his power. If he was to be successful, he needed every ounce of it. His eyes turned crimson, hellfire burning in his chest.

# Chapter Twenty-One

This time it didn't matter who saw him. Seth was done playing human and with the anklet gone, he was a formidable opponent to any force. Granted, he had never considered taking on any of the Macabray siblings before. That didn't mean he couldn't win.

The door flew through the air, landing on the opposite side of the road. Nothing would block him from putting an end to this facade. He stomped into a room lit by hundreds of candles. Their flickering lights reflected the red of the carpet running down the aisle, pews on either side. White flower petals littered the ground—teardrops for the fallen. They led to one place: the altar.

Seth's pace slowed under the strain to the unfolding scene. Three large crosses formed a semicircle around the holy table; a person, back facing forward, strapped to each. They were all naked, motionless and bleeding.

He took stock of the items laid out as ordinarily as if this was a normal every day service. This wasn't the blood and body of their Lord, though. It belonged to the tortured souls tied up— sacrificial lambs.

After all the years Seth had lived, he was sure he had seen the worst evil had to offer. This, however, left him questioning that. He eyed numerous piercings that had been ripped from the flesh, presumably before the real torture began. He barely recognized the two on either side—the smokers from Peters' class. Their greying skin meant it was too late to help either one. They had endured real pain at the hands of a true master. He'd done the one thing that made such agony unbearable. He severed their connection; their bond, their love.

Seth moved to the final cross, Marge. She'd been whipped to the bone—her back would never heal, but she was still alive. He tugged at her bonds carefully, not wanting to inflict any additional pain. Her body fell down limp. He laid her on the floor, covering her with his own shirt, kneeling by her side.

Pain seared through his body from behind. Seth froze on the spot, unable to move an inch. It was ironic, really, it was emotions that were going to cost him his life. He had been so worried about the trio; he hadn't paid attention to what was right behind him.

"Got ya," Jenny snickered, rounding the altar like a cat on the prowl. "You can't do a thing about it, either." She held up his journal. "It provides a detailed explanation on how to use a stake to immobilize a vampire without dealing the final blow," she cackled.

"So Josh and George were telling the truth," Seth said. "You were behind everything all along."

"I'll take care of those two squealers next," Jenny snarled.

Blood dripped from Seth's lips. "There's still one thing I don't understand; what does Peters have to do with all of this?"

Jenny sighed. "I always have to explain it," she said. "I brought Peters here to clear out the bad seeds. At first, it worked wonderfully."

"So what changed?" Seth questioned.

Jenny's nostrils flared. "It was supposed to be about me!" she yelled. "The people we were taking care of were the ones who disagreed with me: hurt me, lied to me, or I plain old didn't like. It took me a year of planning to figure out a way to bring

Peters here. He wasn't satisfied with my enemies, though. He wanted something bigger, more flashy. It became more about evildoers than evil that was done to me. Instead of gaining more control, I was loosing it. I saw his true colours and it was the same as every other person who double-crossed me before."

"Maybe you could sit down and talk it out," Seth joked. "I hear there is a great therapy class held in the basement."

"Ha!" Jenny exclaimed. "I don't need to talk anything out. You saw to that for me." She laughed.

"What do you mean?" Seth asked, feeling the strain of his kneeling position taking its toll on his body. The stake in his back wasn't helping much either.

Jenny threw her head back, allowing fangs to extend before bringing it back to face him again. "I read the section on how to turn a human into an immortal." The book landed on the altar with a thud.

"What did you do?" Seth questioned, horror oozing out his pores. "This isn't a life I would wish on anyone."

"While I had you fetching like a dog, I called Roy," Jenny explained. "He never could say no to me. A few whispers in his ear was all it took."

"You set up the stabbing," Seth muttered.

"That's right," Jenny mused. "Roy got it right for once. He stabbed you right where you couldn't reach."

"What if I was human?" Seth asked. "I'd be dead."

"That's true," Jenny admitted. "How else was I going to find out, though? After you had Roy under control, you naturally turned to me to help remove the dagger."

"There was no one else there," Seth said.

"I pretended I needed to wash up and took it in the bathroom with me," Jenny explained. "Your senses must have been dulled by your lust. You should get that under control, by the way. You didn't even notice. The moment you were gone I licked the blade clean."

"And killed Roy," Seth added.

"I don't need him anymore," Jenny said. "I have the power to take care of haters myself, and it is all thanks to you. You'll be blamed for all of it, of course. I become a fierce immortal. It's a win-win in my book."

"You shouldn't have done that," Seth said. "I didn't write everything in the book. It takes more than ingesting my blood once to change you. In fact, time is ticking before you self-destruct."

"What are you talking about?" Jenny asked, pulling up his chin with a single fingernail.

Seth chuckled. "I don't know what time it is now, but I know it has to be close to the end. Hellfire consumes those who meddle in vampire matters without foreknowledge of the entire process."

Jenny smiled, her finger moving from under his chin to wipe the blood trickling from his mouth. She glanced at the red liquid and then back at the vampire, before seductively plunging it inside her mouth and sucking it clean. "Mm," she hummed. "You betrayed yourself like all the others. You told me I needed a second dose of blood without even realizing it." She took a seat in the front pew.

Seth hung his head. "I knew the moment I saw you, you were the most dangerous person in the room. I should have trusted my first instincts. Tell me, what did you do to Peters?"

"Nothing," the priest answered. "I'm right here." He glanced up at the mess surrounding his altar. "What's the meaning of this?"

# Chapter Twenty-Two

Seth felt both pain and relief at the same time. He glanced over his shoulder at Marge clinging to what was once his white shirt, stained with blood. The stake lay on the ground, inches from her hand. She had saved him. There was no reason for her to intervene; yet she had. Even if he escaped with his life, she most likely wasn't going to be that lucky. Marge had to know that.

From where he knelt, things didn't look good for his own survival. He felt better and could move. Taking on another vampire and a Macabray in full health was a suicide mission. One-on-one at optimal strength, he had a chance. He watched them arguing. There was a chance he could turn them against each other.

"Pardon me," Seth called out. "I was wondering perhaps if I could ask a few questions before I meet my maker."

"Repent before the end," Peters demanded.

"That's where I am confused," Seth admitted. "I thought God was all forgiving. If I swear to follow in his footsteps; change my ways; confess my sins, does he not offer another chance? Does he not welcome me into his house with open arms? Is that not the lesson you were sent here to learn, Macabray?"

The whites in the priest's eyes disappeared, turning pure black. "How do you know of me, mortal?" he bellowed, his voice shaking the foundation.

"He's not a mortal," Jenny said, cackling. "I knew that. He's what you so dearly want to rid this world of, and he was right under your nose the whole time."

"Silence," Peters cried out, his voice amplified by three. A backhand sent Jenny flying across the room. "Tell me who you are, beast. Tell me your name."

"You already know my name," Seth replied, calmly. "This isn't an exorcism. I am not possessed."

"Then tell me what you are," Peters demanded.

It started as a prickling sensation, growing to an itch Seth couldn't scratch. He glanced over his shoulder, at the tattoo on his back, in time to see the wings come to life. They shook free, expanding out on either side. The hole where the stake had been had completely vanished. He rose off the ground, hovering above them.

"NO!" Peters screamed. "Why would He give you wings over me? I have done nothing but rid the world of all that ails it."

"Is it for you to question His choices?" Seth asked. It was all he could think of. A vampire turning into an angel wasn't an everyday occurrence.

Peters' growl was cut short by a side tackle. Jenny blindsided him, knocking him into the organ. It played its final notes in the saddest performance ever made. Jenny stood first, straightening her hair and clothing.

"That takes care of that," Jenny said, slapping her hands against each other. "No one will ever backhand me again." She glanced up at Seth. "Look at you. All pretty and angelic. It doesn't suit you."

"I didn't ask for it," Seth said.

"I still have to kill you," Jenny said.

"Don't think you can get away from me, you little wench," Peters bellowed, pushing pieces of the broken organ off his chest. "What foul creature are you?"

"A vampire," Jenny replied, holding up one finger. "Before you destroy me, though, there is something you should know. Seth is a vampire, too. It's sad that an evil minion without a soul became an angel before you." A grin shadowed her face.

Peters turned to Seth, his face consumed with rage. "Is this true?"

"I must confess my sins," Seth replied. "I am a vampire. I have done things I am not proud of. Most recently I deceived someone."

"You deceived us all," Peters yelled back.

"This went above and beyond normal deception levels, though," Seth explained. "I lied to Jenny."

"What?!" Jenny shrieked.

"I am sorry," Seth continued. "Drinking one dose of blood is what it takes to change a human to vampire. The second is a remedy. Vampires save it for if something goes wrong or someone steals our blood."

"What are you talking about?" Jenny asked, taking a few steps backward, her hand around her throat.

"You can feel it already, can't you?" Seth asked. "There's a heat building, burning you from the inside out."

"What is it?" Jenny asked. "Make it stop."

"Once it has begun, there are only two who can stop it," Seth replied. "I am not one, nor is Peters."

"Hellfire," Peters blurted out. "Only God above and Lucifer below can douse the flames."

"What's happening to me?" Jenny asked, heaving as if she were about to vomit. "It burns." Red flakes danced in her eyes, the pupils vanishing. She screamed as fangs descended fully for the first time.

Peters took a few steps backward, tripping on piece of the organ. He covered his face, watching her jaw hang open.

A sea of lava exploded from her mouth, setting the priest and most of the room a blaze. Jenny ran, making it almost to the back of the building, before collapsing in writhing pain. Her body twitched and convulsed until every last ounce of life had been expelled.

The trail of destruction left in her path, exploded, engulfing floors, walls, and ceiling. Stained-glass windows shattered from the heat. Smoke filled the air.

Peters managed to crawl a few feet before succumbing to the burns. His body turned to ash.

Seth still wasn't fully sure he understood what had happened, but he also wasn't going to stick around to test if he had any new powers. Burning brought a final death to his kind. His fangs told him, whatever else he was; he was still a vampire.

He glanced down, scooping Marge into his arms. She was in rough condition, but one never knew. Perhaps someone would have mercy on her as well.

# Chapter Twenty-Three

*A month later...*

The engine purred as Seth raced down the open highway. He still hadn't made peace with what had happened to him, nor did he understand why. Until he figured that out, nothing else mattered.

The car slowed, pulling into the empty parking lot of a church. Located in the middle of nowhere, it couldn't have gotten very many followers. That suited him just fine. He needed to have a conversation with the big guy, and alone seemed like the easier choice. It was an odd place to look for one's faith, but then again, it was an odd angel doing the seeking. He slammed the door behind him.

Hardwood floors creaked under his weight. The whole parish couldn't have fit more than thirty or forty people. There were no fancy windows or plush red carpets. At the turn of the century it would have been a popular place to pray, though.

His fingers glided over the wood. He took a seat one row back. Clasping his hands together, he laid them on the back of the pew in front, his head bowed down.

"Can I help you?" a man asked.

Seth's head bobbed up. "Father," he replied. "I didn't know anyone was here."

The priest glanced around, his lips curling up into a smile. "There is always someone here," he said. "You have questions about your faith. Perhaps I can help."

"I don't know if anyone can help," Seth admitted. "I lived my whole life thinking I was one thing."

"And now?" the priest questioned, his brow raised.

"Can a person be both bad and good at the same time?" Seth asked, picking up a prayer book.

"Everyone is," the priest answered. "It's what you choose to act on that defines your path."

"What if He," Seth started, glancing up, "chooses you for something, and you aren't sure he made the right choice. Can He make a mistake?"

"He," the priest replied, mimicking Seth's actions of looking upward, "tends to know what He is doing. We have to trust Him on that front. It's called faith. Then again, maybe He made His biggest mistake in creating man. He hasn't given up on them yet, though."

"Why am I having such a hard time with all of this?" Seth asked. "Shouldn't it be easier?"

"You have a slew of emotions you don't know what to do with, battling each other inside," the priest explained. "It's normal for you to question what you are feeling. When you let the love in through religion, it warms your heart as if you were in love with another person. That can be confusing."

"Is that what I was feeling?" Seth asked. "I thought I was in love with a woman. It seemed so real."

"Love always feels real," the priest answered. "You need to ask yourself what you truly felt for her. Was it love or lust or something else?"

"I guess it is easier to see looking back," Seth admitted. "I felt the emotion in the church first. I assumed it was her. Why wouldn't it be, I was attracted to her, after all? It didn't make sense when I didn't know more than her name and figure."

"Then I think you have your answer. I'll leave you to think in peace. Remember He," the priest said pointing up at the ceiling, "is always here to talk if you need Him."

"Father," Seth replied, "does He know what is going to happen next?"

"He always has a plan," the priest replied. "Only we can carry out that plan, though. We all have our part to play."

"Father," Seth called out, not wanting him to leave before he asked one more question. "How do I know what the plan is?"

"He always gives us signs," the priest replied. "All you have to do is watch for them and open up to the possibilities."

Seth put his head down, contemplating the old man's words. They made sense. He had pulled over at that very church on a whim.

"Sir," a woman's voice called out.

Seth turned around, coming face-to-face with a young officer. "Yes, ma'am," he replied.

"You can't be in here, sir," the officer said. "This building isn't safe."

"It's a church," Seth argued. He glanced around, seeing things in a different light. Even the pew he was sitting on was covered in an inch of dust.

"It's been abandoned for years," the office replied. "You need to leave now." She inched closer, one hand on her sidearm.

Seth held up his hands. "I'm going," he said. He made his way down the aisle, passing the officer without incident. "What about the priest?"

"There is no priest here, sir," the officer said.

"I was just talking to him," Seth argued. "I thought he was reopening the place."

"My partner is sweeping the rest of the building," she replied. "If anyone else is here, we'll find them."

Seth stepped outside into the sunlight. Since his transformation it no longer aged his skin. A true miracle for his kind, but one he had no one to share it with. "Mind if I wait to see if you find him? He was nice old man. I'd hate to see something happen to him."

"Suit yourself, sir," the office said. "I could charge you with trespassing, but seeing as you were praying and not destroying, I'm letting you off with a warning. Don't let it happen again."

"No, ma'am," Seth replied, turning over a sign that had fallen down on the lawn. The corners of his lips curled upward. "Well, I'll be..." He stopped short of saying damned.

"Is something wrong?" the office asked.

"No, ma'am," Seth answered. "Do you happen to know if this place is still for sale? I might be interested in buying it."

"It sure is," the office said, pulling up her trousers. "I just happen to be the agent. I dabble in real estate in my time off." She handed him a card.

"Everything okay over there?" her partner called.

"Yeah," she yelled back. "This here fella might be interested in buying the place. Did you find anyone else?"

"Nope," he replied. "No one other than the woman sitting in his car."

Seth spun around. He had arrived alone and expected to be leaving alone as well. The passenger door opened. The last person he expected to see stepped out.

"Is she with you?" the officer asked.

"Yes," Seth replied. "We are going in the same direction."

"All right," the office replied. "We didn't find anyone else. He must have gotten out the back and took off. You give me a call if you decide to purchase the place."

"I will," Seth agreed, his eyes still locked on the woman standing by his car. "Is there a motel in town? I'd like to sleep on it and discuss it with my partner."

"There sure is," the office said. "Two miles up on the left. They are thinking of selling, too. In case you might be looking for multiple investment opportunities in the area." She opened the door to her car. "I got other calls to attend to. Make sure you are gone before we head back this way."

"Yes, ma'am," Seth agreed, adding a nod. He strolled back to his car, trying to find the right words. "I didn't expect to see you again."

"I didn't expect to be seen again," Marge answered. "Someone thought you could use a companion, and we might be a good fit."

"He's not big on subtlety when it comes to signs, is He?" Seth mused. "You look good."

"Reincarnation does that to a girl," Marge giggled. "Thank you for trying to save me. I never had the chance to say that before."

"As I recall, I should be thanking you," Seth suggested.

"I think turning into an angel would have taken care of the stake," Marge mused. "Call it a hunch."

Seth smiled. "So are you..."

"An angel too? Yup, and I have the wings to prove it," Marge admitted. "Looks like you're stuck with me."

"That might not be so bad," Seth replied, smiling. "I think He might just know what He's doing, after all."

"So where to?" Marge asked, getting back in the car.

"Down the street," Seth answered, "to the motel."

"Hey," Marge complained, "what type of an angel do you take me for?" She chuckled.

"We can afford separate rooms," Seth mused, adding, "for now."

"For now?" she asked.

"Until we get to know each other better," Seth said. "We have all of eternity to fall in love, after all."

Marge smiled. "I like that idea," she admitted, resting her feet on the dashboard. "I like it a lot."

Seth shook his head. "I hope God knows what He's getting into recruiting us."

Marge laughed. "I think He does. We both have a second chance to make things right, and we make a good pair."

"To second chances," Seth said. "Speaking of which, I've decided. I am buying that church. I think I can fix it up."

"Don't you mean we?" Marge complained.

"Yeah, I guess I do," Seth said. "It's going to take some getting used to. I've been alone for a very long time."

"Well, you don't have to be anymore," Marge said, reclining her seat back. "From now on, we face the world together."

"I like that," Seth said. "I like that a lot."

"I have a feeling this is the beginning of some of the greatest adventures of all times," Marge said. "I like not knowing what comes next."

Seth nodded. "Keep your eyes open for signs. I have a feeling it won't be long before we have our first official assignment. Until then, I guess we enjoy the ride."

# *Author's Message*

I hope you enjoyed reading In A Heart Beat as much as I did writing it.

If you are interested in reading more about Seth & Marge, please leave a review to let me know!

Until next time... happy reading!

# ABOUT THE AUTHOR

C.A. King is the recipient of several awards, including: The Hamilton Spectator Readers' Choice Award for 2017 & 2018 Best Author; The Brant News Readers' Choice Award for 2017 Best Author; Readers' Favorite award in the short story/novella category; the 2017 SIBA Award for Best New Adult; the 2017 SIBA Award for Best Novella; 2018 Readers' Favorite International Book Awards: Gold Medal in the Fiction - Supernatural genre; and 2018 Readers' Favorite International Book Awards: Bronze Medal in the Fiction - New Adult genre

Currently residing in Brantford, Ontario Canada, she lives with her two sons. She began her writing career after the tragic loss of her parents and husband. Redirecting her emotions through writing became therapeutic in her battle with depression and in 2014 she decided to publish some of her works.

# Other Titles from C.A. King

## The Portal Prophecies

These great titles in C.A. King's The Portal Prophecies series are available now at most online book retailers:

*A Keeper's Destiny*

*A Halloween's Curse*

*Frost Bitten*

*Sleeping Sands*

*Deadly Perceptions*

*Finding Balance*

*Volume I (Books 1-3)*

*Volume II (Books 4-6)*

The prophecies are the key to their survival. Can they solve them in time?

## Shattering the Effects of Time

Join the Shinning brothers, Jessie, Dezi and Pete as they set out on a quest to save their younger sister. No magic known to them or their friends has ever been able to reverse the grip of time. A few legends, however, exist mentioning ancient items that may hold the key to do exactly that.

This brand new series will take you on a search for the Fountain of Youth and Mermaids; a quest for the Holy Grail; a trip to visit Daryl the mountain guru, in the hunt for the Cinamani Stone; on a search for Ambrosia, the food of the Gods; and other adventures.

*Surviving the Sins:*

The prophecies are being rewritten. This time someone is using the seven deadly sins: Lust; Gluttony; Greed; Sloth; Wrath; Envy; and Pride, to unlock an ancient evil. The book falls into Jade's hands to answer destiny's call. Can she survive the sins?

*Book 1: Answering the Call*

*Book 2: Pride*

*Book 3: Lust*

*Book 4: Gluttony*

*Book 5: Wrath*

*Book 6: Envy*

*Book 7: Sloth*

*Book 8: Greed*

## When Leaves Fall: A Different Point of View Story

Ralph wakes up to what others only experience in a nightmare. Chained to a shed, he has no idea where he is, or who his captor is. His memories a blurred at best. As the days press on he finds himself experiencing a roller coaster of feelings. Hunger, thirst and pain become his only companions. Flashbacks of a happier time are all he has to keep him going. As his situation deteriorates, he finds himself doubting the very things he wants most -- a family.

*When Leaves Fall* is a dramatic-thriller with a twist. Keep the tissue box close for the ending.

## Tomoiya's Story

A Vampire Tale. She had a secret but she wasn't the only one who had something to hide.

Book I ~ Escape to Darkness

Book II ~ Collecting Tears

Book III~ Coming Soon

## Peach Coloured Daisies: A Cursed by the Gods Story

He couldn't die. An ancient curse meant she always did. This time, that was going to change -- one way or another.

When Daisy's grandmother, her last living relative, passes away, she doesn't know where to turn. Things go from bad to worse when a local psychic tells her about a curse. Alone and confused, she ends up in front of her college professor's office, ready to cry her heart out in his arms.

Matt Demi might be the son of a God, but he's living the life of a cursed man. He's had to watch the woman he loves die on her twenty-first birthday countless times. Nothing he does seems to be able to affect the outcome. When she shows up at his office scared out of her wits by a psychic's prediction, he vows this time will be different.

With only three days, Matt will need to embrace a side of him he swore off long ago to save her, but will he lose himself in the process?

## Flower Shields: A Four Horsemen Novel

Meet the four horsemen: Michael, Gabrielle, Uriel and Raphael. For centuries their job has been to guard the gates of hell, making sure they never open. Without the keys, there was never any real threat. That's about to change. There are rumours on the horizon that demon followers unearthed scrolls that explain exactly how to find the lost keys. This new battle is a race to see which side locates them first.

Michael couldn't care less about the love story behind how and why the world was created. In fact, nothing matters to him other than keeping the gates to hell closed. If one of the lost keys ever fell into the wrong hands, all humanity would be doomed. He's not going to let that happen -- at any cost.

*********

Tara's life is nothing short of a disaster. She's managed to flunk out of college with about the same amount of dignity as every relationship she's been in. The only constant in her life has been her love for flowers. When she's attacked at work, a stranger comes to her aid. Michael might be good-looking, but he's also arrogant, bossy and crazy. He's also her only chance to figure out who attacked her and why. Should she follow her heart and trust him -- or listen to her head and run?

*Drawing Strength From Words: A Four Horsemen Novel*

Meet the four horsemen: Michael, Gabrielle, Uriel and Raphael.

For centuries their sole purpose has been guarding the sealed gates to hell. Without keys, there was never any real threat. That was about to change...

For Gabrielle, protecting mankind was merely a job for which she received little credit. The vast insecurities of men altered history itself, portraying her as a masculine brute. Taking a back seat to her brothers seemed the right thing to do, but left a bitter taste in her mouth and an impenetrable barricade shielding her heart.

\*\*\*\*\*\*\*\*\*\*

Ryder bounced around the system from the moment both his parents were killed. Between that and run-ins with the law for crimes he never committed, it seemed the whole world was conspiring against him. Never growing attached to anyone was rule number one: a rule he'd never broken until a white-haired vixen, with blocks of ice on her shoulders, walked right into his life. Melting through those frosty layers became all that mattered, even if that meant sacrificing himself in the process.

## Hitting The High Note: A Four Horsemen Novel

Meet the four horsemen, Michael, Gabrielle, Uriel, and Raphael. For centuries their sole purpose has been guarding the sealed gates to hell. Without keys, there was never any real threat. That was about to change...

Uriel could pass for a cowboy – straight out of an aftershave commercial – at least in appearance. With a trusty lasso at his side, he'll take on all comers in a fight to the finish in order to prove his worth. There's no heading home empty-handed, when he already lives in the shadows of his siblings. A couple of days and a handful of puns is all he needs to make sure that doesn't happen.

Bekka knows exactly what it's like to be invisible and has her best friend, Veronica, to thank for it. All her life, she's been too frightened to take a chance, especially when it came to her music and love. A chance meeting with a cowboy, and then a gentleman, turns her world upside down, leaving her with a choice that changes all of their lives.

Personalities clash and secrets are revealed in this third instalment of the Four Horsemen Series.

## Miracles Not Included

A heartfelt romantic story about: life; love; loss; and learning to love again. If only life came with instructions and a warning label ~ Miracles Not Included.

**********

Chris was born to be a writer. Even the smallest of details couldn't pass without notice, often becoming part of a plot for her next novel. The one thing she never saw coming was her husband's sudden illness.

Jason loved his wife from the moment they met. Nothing could ever change that -- nothing except the death sentence he'd been handed -- a terminal cancer diagnosis.

His story was ending: Hers was starting a new chapter and more than one miracle was needed to turn the page.

## Twisted Tales of a Dead End Street

A paranormal mystery laced with comedic undertones: Twisted Tales of a Dead End Street.

Nine neighbours were invited to the mysterious dinner party at 9 Nine Street. Their host, the owner of the mansion, had more planned for the evening than just roast beef.

When the secret of their quiet street was revealed, everything changed, blurring the lines between the tangible and the paranormal.

Was the number nine the difference between life and death? Would any of them survive long enough to uncover the truth? They would each soon find out this wasn't a simple case of who-done-it so much as one of what was being done and by whom.

## Shot Through The Heart: A Faerie Tale

A tale of two worlds -- one filled with magic; the other void of it. But what happened to those trapped between the two? Adelia was about to find out...

Magic and structure were the foundations of her existence. Temptation controlled the ability to destroy everything she knew. The world of men held a powerful allure over her heart, waking that which had long been dormant. It enticed her, snagging her in a web of emotions.

A decision had to be made. Was feeling love for the first time worth sacrificing magic and immortality?

## Do Not Open Until Halloween

When eighteen year old Caitlin agreed to babysit her eccentric Aunt's two cats and house, she had no idea that Justin was finally going to ask her for a date the same weekend. Torn between family and crush, she chose to take her best friends' suggestion to heart, arranging a small Friday night gathering. Little did she know a fairy was about to crash the party with trouble hot on her wings.

Caitlin will have to dig deep to find even a smidgen of belief in magic or there won't be any hope of saving her new friend from being hunted.

In this young adult fantasy, award-winning author, C.A. King, explores the answer to one of the questions readers have always wanted to ask...

Where do fairies come from?

### Truly Unfortunate

Growing up in Knoll County wasn't easy, especially without any childhood memories. Truly spent her whole life searching for the answers her mind refused to reveal. There might have been horrors in her past, but her current existence wasn't much better than a nightmare. After beginning treatments with a new doctor, disturbing visions began to resurface. The stench of death surrounded her, but where exactly was it coming from?

Jeff always knew he wanted to be one of Knoll County's finest and had no problem achieving that dream. A part of his ambition stemmed from the death of a classmate at the tender age of nine. It might have been ruled an accident, but his gut told him otherwise. When people start turning up dead in the same pattern, Jeff will be forced to put everything on the line to connect the dots between past and present. But in doing so, will his own future be jeopardized?

Truly Unfortunate is a dark paranormal thriller that will leave readers with chills after answering the question: Which is stronger... the boundaries of reality or the safety on one's own mind?

## *Merry Apocalypse*

For centuries, families gathered throughout the holiday season to hear recitals of the famous words of Dr. Clement C. Moore's 'Twas the Night Before Christmas and celebrate the long awaited return of Santa. His jovial generosity became synonymous with all that was Merry and bright. Then everything changed.

This year, the gatherings are sharing their own Christmas story. Merry Apocalypse includes the telling of a new traditional tale that echoes the tone and rhythm of familiar poetry, but instead of joy and bliss, contains warnings of danger and death.

### Sometimes Love Stinks

What's in a name? Everything when it's laughable.

Gastrella M. Balance was living a never-ending nightmare. For several years, she'd been the butt of jokes about... her butt. Moving to Knollville was a chance for a fresh start. It was a place where no one knew her past, or her name and she was determined to keep both a secret. Her strategy was to stay under the radar and as inconspicuous as possible. That plan, however, went south the first time she laid eyes on Tanner. When he noticed her, too, she couldn't help but hope for a bit of romance, no matter how far fetched it seemed.

*****

Tanner had everything a guy could ask for in his senior year of high school. He had a football in one hand and a pretty girl hanging off the other arm. Being popular and the centre of attention came naturally to him. Taking tests, however, did not and he was desperate to keep that part of his life to himself.

When a series of pranks go awry, they'll both be faced with confronting their personal anxieties. Together, they might have a chance to overcome the odds and survive the year.

Sometimes Love Stinks is a romantic comedy that deals with issues that are both real and difficult. While the main characters in this story are from the mundane world, readers can expect to find the signature supernatural kiss C.A. King adds to all her books.

www.ingramcontent.com/pod-product-compliance
Lightning Source LLC
Chambersburg PA
CBHW031112260626
47172CB00001B/334